I0618150

OTZI'S CURSE

MARY JUNE

This is a work of fiction. Names, characters, places, and incidents are products of the author's imagination or are used fictitiously and are not to be construed as real. Any resemblance to actual events, locations, organizations, or persons, living or dead, is entirely coincidental.

World Castle Publishing, LLC
Pensacola, Florida

Copyright © Mary June 2016
Paperback ISBN: 9781629894461
eBook ISBN: 9781629894478
First Edition World Castle Publishing, LLC, April 18, 2016
http://www.worldcastlepublishing.com

Licensing Notes
All rights reserved. No part of this book may be used or reproduced in any manner whatsoever without written permission, except in the case of brief quotations embodied in articles and reviews.

Cover: Karen Fuller
Editor: Maxine Bringenberg

CHAPTER 1

"And how is this relevant to *you*?"

The professor glared around the crowded room and two dozen pairs of eyes fastened themselves quickly on their notes. The room was darkened to accommodate the overhead projector, and the solitary light gleaming off the instructor's glasses created a rather sinister mood.

High school juniors from all over California had rolled in for the Berkeley Summer Session, a feat accomplished only after surviving the rigorous entrance requirements and beating out countless others with their grade point average. They were the cream of the crop. And those gathered into Professor Shield's cramped course on genetics and society half-believed the hardest part was behind them. They were greatly mistaken.

"*Think* people! There is a reason why you're here."

Gene Barfield scrolled rapidly through his dimmed MacBook, re-reading the notes they'd taken for the last hour. The subject of today's lecture had been Otzi, an ice corpse discovered in Italy in 1991. From an anthropological standpoint he was a rare find, and scientists had been able to garner a wealth of information from his frozen body.

They'd determined that Otzi was about forty-five years old when he died, weighing one-hundred and ten pounds and standing a little over five feet tall. He suffered from whipworms and fleas, as well as osteoarthritis of the hip. Stress during the last months of his life had created ridges in his fingernails. The smoky fires to cook his food and keep him warm had darkened his lungs. Missing from birth were his twelfth pair of ribs, as well as his wisdom teeth. Lyme disease from ticks had weakened his joints. Modern studies had even revealed Otzi's final meal based on the contents of his digestive tract; a meager feast of goat meat and barley.

But what was so significant about Otzi was that his DNA was completely absent in modern European populations. The very fabric of the Iceman's genetic make-up matched no living being. He was historically, scientifically, and fundamentally alone.

A fact that lent a small note of irony to the teacher's targeted question.

"Mr. Barfield!"

Gene jumped in his chair and stared back into the ghoulish eyes of his professor.

"How is this relevant to you?"

The irony faded and Gene's mind raced as he peered tentatively up from his laptop. "Because it will be on the final?"

He was rewarded with a rare smile. "Yes." Shields walked back to the white board and flipped on the lights. "Because all this information will be present on your final. You must be able to identify the specific genetic markers that make Otzi an anomaly today." He raised his voice as the bell rang and kids started packing up and shuffling to the door.

"By now you should have a good idea for the thesis of your research papers, people! They're 75 percent of your grade!"

Gene flooded out with the rest of the students, blinking in the bright summer sun, and piled his things into his new Jeep Wrangler, a birthday gift from his parents. All Wranglers had interchangeable tops, so this was the best birthday gift, in Gene's opinion. He could take off the top in a jiffy and drive through the beautiful hills with the breeze tousling his hair. The car gave him the freedom to attend classes while still living at home where he could thrive on love, laundry, and home-cooked meals. The holy trinity to the modern teenage boy. It also came with a few other perks....

"Bye, Gene."

Gene paused in appreciative silence as Samantha Wren pushed her long red hair off her creamy shoulder. His eyes lingered a moment on her thin camisole before travelling up to return her bright smile.

"See you tomorrow, Sam."

He hopped into the driver's seat and sped away before he might appear too interested, and before Samantha could see the embarrassing flush spreading across his cheeks.

As he sailed down the familiar streets back to his childhood home in the Berkeley Hills, he couldn't help but smile. The "Personal Relevance of Otzi." It had a nice ring to it. Perhaps he would use it for his term paper. He pulled into his driveway and jumped out, still smiling. At the very least, he would finally have something to talk about with his father.

"Gene, take off your shoes and help us in the kitchen! You're just in time for dinner!"

Gene sighed in resignation and ditched his shoes in the entryway. Scarcely home two seconds and he already had chores. He made his way quickly into the kitchen, where his stepmother Maren and little sister Sophie were fussing about over a steaming casserole. He lifted his hand in greeting to Maren and flashed a grin at Sophie. She had that martyred, tortured expression she got whenever she was asked to help with housework.

Maren glanced up with a faint welcoming smile. "How was school? You had...genetics today, right?" Before he could answer, she returned to her work. "Do me a favor and get your father from his study, okay? We're eating on the porch."

Gene wandered down the hallway and paused automatically outside his father's door. Although Adam Barfield had been using this study ever since Gene could remember, he always got a little nervous before going inside. To say his father was secretive about his work would be massively understating it. Once, when Gene was six or seven, the door had been unlocked and his father had come home to find Gene playing with his dinosaurs on the floor inside. That was the first time he'd ever heard his father swear. He'd been so terrified, he remembered his nanny had had to come and carry him out.

Gene shook his head as the images faded away, and decided to knock.

"What is it?" came the abrupt reply from inside.

"It's me," Gene answered cautiously. "Mom says it's time for dinner. We're eating outside."

There was a shuffling and the sound of a chair creaking backwards as his father stood. "I'll be there in a minute...I just need to finish up in here."

Gene joined the girls out on the patio. It was a balmy summer evening, an event never to be squandered in the Bay Area. As he took his seat across from Sophie, Gene looked out across the yard to hills stretching out from beneath them. If he squinted, he could just barely make out the faint gleam of the ocean sparkling in the distance.

The door opened and shut as Adam rushed out to join them. He was still wearing his white coat from the lab, and his fingers were smeared with the ink of countless pens. Gene noted these details with a small sigh. His father had been known to bring his work home with him.

"Sorry." Adam cast an apologetic glance at Maren as he pulled out his chair and settled down. "I didn't mean to make you wait."

She gave him a tight smile and began dishing out the casserole. Across the table, Sophie caught Gene's attention and discreetly rolled her eyes. He stifled a smile. He and his sister weren't supposed to know that their parents weren't in love with each other anymore. They were at the age where most adults assumed the information would be too damaging. Gene thought back and tried to remember if there had ever been a time when Maren and Adam were truly affectionate. He couldn't think of anything. His childhood was a hazy blur, and the only dynamic he could remember strongly was the presence of three women, not just Maren.

"So Dad," Gene began proudly, eager to share his new wealth of scientific knowledge. "Today in class we—"

"Did you ever get that follow-up to the World Health Organization?" Maren interrupted. Gene fell silent and began quietly playing with his food.

Adam looked up from his wine. "Yes Maren, I did."

It sounded like more of a challenge than an answer, and all four members of the Barfield family busied themselves with the art of acting casual. Performances like this were turning into the normal dinner routine. Perhaps Gene would start eating on campus.

Sophie twirled her fork, then ostentatiously let it crash noisily onto her plate, making the other three jump. "I went to the beach today with Kim."

Maren smiled at her indulgently, while Adam gave that robotic nod that his family knew meant he didn't care or he wasn't really listening. Gene looked at Sophie with a touch of sympathy. In a lot of ways, she was the lucky kid. Maren adored her, she had a teeming circle of friends, and financially speaking, she could probably have just about anything she wanted.

Except the attention of her father.

As much as Gene often felt slighted by Adam, he no longer craved his affections the way Sophie still did. It was depressing to watch her try night after night, only to be rebuked and ignored.

"That's cool." Gene tried to help. "Which one's Kim again? The one with the nose ring?"

Sophie rolled her eyes. Big brothers could be so stupid sometimes. "Mandy's the one with the nose ring. Kim's the one with the tattoo on her wrist." She said this proudly, as if her group of suburban princesses had upped their street-cred with a bit of henna. "In fact," she looked at Adam significantly, "I was thinking of getting one myself."

Maren dropped her fork. "Oh no you will not, young lady! Adam, talk to her!"

Adam looked up blankly from his salad. "What?"

"A *tattoo*?" Maren prompted.

"Oh, right." Adam returned absentmindedly to his meal. "No, Gene, you can't get a tattoo."

Sophie growled. "We were talking about *me*, Dad."

"Actually," Gene leaned forward, trying to break the tension, "I had a really interesting lecture in my genetics class today. Dad, have you ever heard of a guy called 'Otzi?'"

10

Red wine poured over the white table cloth, soaking the remnants of the casserole and staining Maren's starched pencil skirt on the other side.

"Adam!" she shrieked as everyone leapt to their feet. They grabbed their napkins and began dabbing uselessly at the ruined meal.

But Adam was a statue. He remained frozen in his chair, pale as a sheet, gripping the arm rests with white knuckles as the wine trickled around him. His eyes were fixed on Gene.

"What did you say?" he breathed.

Gene turned to his father with a confused frown, trying to remember what they'd been talking about as he simultaneously restrained the dogs from licking up the alcohol.

"Otzi." It finally came back to him. "I just asked if you'd ever heard of the mummy, Otzi."

"Adam, are you going to help us here?!"

Adam came out of his trance, blinking at Maren before he leapt to his feet. "Yes, sorry! It's okay everyone, we'll just move dinner inside. Gene—keep the dogs back. Sophie, help your mother with the plates."

Dinner was a more subdued affair than normal, and no one spoke as they choked down the soggy wine-infused casserole. At one point Sophie muttered to no one in particular that she was going to get buzzed. Afterwards, Gene and Adam volunteered to clean up as a fuming Maren went to shower and change.

Neither one said much as Adam washed the dishes and Gene dried them. In fact, they had just about finished when Adam suddenly turned off the water.

"So that's what you're studying in genetics these days?" he asked with seeming disinterest. "Otzi and other such finds?"

Gene finished drying the plate in his hands. "Yeah. Do you know anything about it?"

Adam was a neuroscientist at Berkeley, and topics of a scientific nature were the only things Gene had found that they could ever manage to bond over.

"I know a bit," Adam admitted, leaning back against the counter.

In fact, he knew more than a bit, and as they talked Gene was amazed at the stores of information his father held on the topic. They not only analyzed the peculiarities of Otzi's K1ö subhaplogroup, but speculated as to whether he could truly have left no genetic mark, wondering if all the inhabitants in the villages where he was discovered had been tested.

The conversation took them well into the evening, and by the time Gene glanced at the clock and realized the time, it could have ranked as one of their longest discussions on record.

"I've got to go!" he exclaimed, jumping up from his chair and pulling on his jacket. "I told the guys I'd meet them at the basketball courts for a game."

"Yes…you should go," Adam murmured, getting to his feet as Gene disappeared down the hall.

***

As he stared around the empty kitchen, he was flushed with a surreal kind of excitement, though his skin was oddly cool. Of all the things Gene could have come home with…*Otzi*?!

At first Adam had been panicked, almost sick with nerves, but the more he thought about it now, the more he wanted to smile. It was behind them. Otzi was as bad as it could get—and it was *over*. Nothing else could ever come close.

Adam rubbed his eyes in absurd relief and found himself chuckling. "So what are you doing for your next unit?" he asked, wandering down the hall to see Gene off.

Gene zipped up his jacket and headed out with a parting wave. "Next week we're testing each other's DNA."

He didn't see his father sink slowly onto the stairs, clutching his chest. He didn't see the look of terror that grayed his hair and whitened his features, aging him in a single instant.

Testing each other's DNA.

Adam breathed hard through his nose, grabbing onto the banister for support as the room around him tilted and swayed.

As bad as things could get?

No.

Things were about to get a whole lot worse....

Chapter 2

The day had begun like any other. Adam strapped on his backpack and mountain gear before embarking on a seventeen mile hike through the Otztal Alps. The weather was relatively good and visibility was clear. It was the perfect ending to his Italian sabbatical.

But in reality, the significance of the day predated both Adam and Italy. It harkened back to 3255 BC, when the Iceman nibbled his last berry and ate sparingly of dried meat. Exhausted and marginally nourished, he laid out his weapons and pack, pillowed his head on a flat rock, and fell into an endless sleep. Five thousand years later, Adam Barfield arrived on the scene.

He panted and gasped as he hiked. Perhaps, in hindsight, he had overestimated his athleticism. A seventeen mile hike looked great on paper, but in reality, it was taking its toll. Nevertheless, the alpine quiet was exactly the kind of solace for which Adam had been searching when he planned this retreat several months ago. There was something about the solitude that comforted him. It was most likely the exact reason that at home, he gravitated towards his lab. Nothing soothed the spirit like silence.

Static from the portable shortwave receiver shattered Adam's reverie and jarred his pleasantly rested senses. Georg Laich of the Austrian Broadcasting Service was relating a press release.

"A recently discovered body at the Hauslabjoch, below the Finailspitze, is reputed to be at least one hundred and fifty years old. The corpse seems to be very well preserved. In his hand, the dead man holds an axe."

Adam paused on the trail as his mind flooded with the same rush of images ingrained in every child who grew up watching the History Channel. The Hauslabjoch wasn't very far. If Adam hurried, he could mostly likely glimpse the mummy before the proper officials were dispatched to collect the body. In a fit of excitement, he flattened his map and conferred with his compass before taking off at top speed towards the excavation.

Only serendipity could be responsible for the events that followed.

As Adam approached the site, he found it deserted. The last of the recovery crew had been ordered away. At the same time, the heat of the day had produced maximal thawing, and as it was coming on dusk, the refreezing had not yet begun. As both a scientist and a child of multimedia DVDs, this was the perfect opportunity to see a bit of history up close in person. Glancing around behind him, Adam crept closer to the ice. Then he saw it.

Time seemed to suspend as Adam stared at the primitive man. The man stared back. The evening paused, and for a quiet moment, it was just the two of them.

A collision of history. A joining of two worlds. A brief intertwining in the fabric of time.

Adam's next acts seemed preordained. He would never be able to explain or understand them.

With the speed and precision of a scientist, he knelt by the exposed body, meticulously scrutinizing the condition of the dead man's skin and flesh. He made a mental note of the scattered artifacts, as well as the hacking and brutal attempts that had been made to free the Iceman from his frigid grave.

Then, with a compulsion beyond his control, Adam's hands moved of their own accord into his pocket to extract his Swiss army knife. He glanced up into the hollowed eyes of the mummy.

"Hold on, buddy. This won't hurt a bit!"

He flipped open the blade and plunged his hands into the icy meltwater around the partially submerged Iceman. With barely a pause, he incised a small slit into the scrotum, then gently pressed with thumb and forefinger until the testicles slipped into his waiting palm. After a quick appraisal, he carefully wrapped the well-preserved glands and tubes and placed the bundle into his fanny pack, further protecting it with shards of ice.

The second he was finished, Adam backed swiftly away within the tree-line. He was breathing as though he had just run a marathon, but his hands were steady and his face was calm. He waited a moment, mind reeling from the implications of what he'd done, but there were no sirens. No armed men came running with clubs and shields to arrest him. There were only the muted sounds of twilight and the steady drip of water trickling off the mummy's icy sternum.

It was time to leave.

With an all-out effort, Adam reached the Similaun refuge by nightfall. There, he located a niche near a small outbuilding where he dug into the ice and snow and stashed his fanny pack. He carefully mounded the cache with chunks of ice until it resembled a small igloo, thus preserving the fragile contents. Reluctant to leave the precious bundle behind but seeing no alternative, he hurried to his overnight lodgings.

If Adam was hoping to make a discreet, anonymous departure from Italy, he was sadly disappointed. From the moment he entered the hut he was the center of attention. An American travelling alone in an area this remote was bound to get people talking. Almost immediately several other guests introduced themselves in the Austrian tradition, including their titles and occupations, although they did not relinquish their spots before the cozy fire.

Not to be outshone, Adam replied jovially, "What a relief to be here! That trail's a bitch after dark." Several of the older men chuckled and made room for him to sit beside the fire. "I'm Adam Barfield, Professor of Neuroscience at the University of California Medical School in Berkeley. I've been travelling on sabbatical, but the academic year is due to start and I'm ready to get back to the classroom." There were vague affirmations and approvals, when without any graceful segue, Adam blurted, "So what have you heard about the man in the ice?"

Discretion be damned! Adam had a scientific gold mine sitting in an igloo a stone's throw away. He had to talk to someone about it.

As he brought Adam a pint of beer, Markus Pirpamer, the inn's proprietor, asked, "Have you seen our Iceman? How did you learn of the find?"

Nodding his thanks for the beer, Adam responded hastily, "No, I didn't see him. I heard about the discovery on a radio broadcast on my way here. It's a fascinating story, but the signal kept cutting in and out. I couldn't get many of the details."

With no greater invitation than that, the atmosphere of the room seemed to literally inflate with the abundance of answers and egos. It seemed each guest was an expert in some field related to the discovery of the Iceman; either an anthropologist or an allied discipline, or an expert in glacial rescue. In rapid order Adam learned the corpse was at least four thousand years old, that he had died from exposure, and that he was a Bronze Age shepherd of around thirty-five to forty. Furthermore, he had been given an official name, a moniker combining "Otztal" and "yeti."

Otzi.

The room buzzed in excited speculation as they poured over the details. Many bodies had been recovered in this same way, but they had been modern skiing and hiking victims, released by the snows as Otzi had been. The authorities had been accustomed to notifying relatives and having the bodies claimed. Now they were facing challenging questions.

How would Otzi be preserved? To what government would he belong; had he been found in Italy or Austria? What could be learned about this man from his body and equipment?

Adam, too, was involved in deep speculation. As he heard these speculative questions, his brain was churning out questions of his own.

How would he get his treasure safely back to California? Would it be possible to keep the origins of his future data a secret? Had he really just stolen a man's testes?

Tired, and eager to be alone with his plans, he excused himself and headed up the stairs to his modest bunkroom, where he slept a solid nine hours.

Dawn was cold and forbidding, but Adam was too uneasy to notice. His only thought was to rescue his prize from the makeshift freezer and escape to Vent unnoticed.

There was hardly anyone about, but that didn't stop Adam from looking over his shoulder every few seconds as he made his way back to the igloo. He was immensely relieved to find everything waiting exactly how he'd left it. The invaluable bundle was nestled snugly in the ice, and the vitals inside appeared undisturbed.

Tucking the packet deep into his jacket pocket, Adam hurried into town. He made his connection to Innsbruck as scheduled, but instructed his driver to stop at a FedEx office along the way. A package like this wouldn't exactly make it through customs.

Warm air blew into his face the second he opened the door, and he elbowed his way to the front of the short line, worried about the cellular damage to the sample in these temperatures.

"Excuse me!" huffed a middle-aged woman as Adam shoved roughly in front of her. Her three small children glared in perfect unison and Adam caught his breath before clutching involuntarily at the package in his hands.

"I'm so sorry." His mind raced, creating on the spot. "It's my wife, you see. She's not well. I really need to get this to her as soon as possible."

Adam's face must have been quite a sight, because the woman softened before graciously stepping back and offering him her place in line. He thanked her profusely and placed his prize gently on the counter.

The cashier glanced up with supreme disinterest and set it on the scale. "And what will we be shipping today?"

"Simian organs," Adam replied.

The woman behind him gave him a strange look, and he twiddled his thumbs innocently as the paperwork was produced.

FedEx could guarantee dry ice conditions, a necessity reiterated by Adam no less than seven times. The package would be hand delivered to the Berkeley tissue bank — no customs, no delay, and no danger of deterioration. After exasperating everyone in the store with his incessant repetitions, Adam headed for the airport feeling confident his little miracle would survive.

An hour later, he settled his rangy frame into the slightly cramped airline seat. The last two days had been the most emotionally exhausting of his life, and he was more than ready to lean back, close his eyes, and give his tired mind a rest.

Then a falling projectile struck him on the head.

"Oh! Pardon me!"

Adam flinched and handed the oversized bag back to a small, rounded woman who struggled to stuff it into the overhead compartment. Adam listened to her grunts, sighs, and "oh-mys" as long as he decently could before getting up to give her a hand.

"Oh, you're so kind and gentlemanly!" she gushed as he crammed the parcel into the farthest corner and slammed the lid shut. "And *oh* — so very good-looking too! You must be returning from some athletic, outdoor, sporty thing to look so fit and strong!"

He flashed her a tight smile and returned to his seat, hoping she'd get the message and leave him to enjoy the rest of the flight in peace.

There was a grating creak as she settled her rotund frame into the seat beside him.

"I'm Elsie Conway, and I've been abroad for the last two weeks. I can't wait to get back to San Pablo and tell all my friends about my travels abroad."

Adam resisted the urge to cringe. He had been planning on using the flight time to rest and plan the next critical moves in his preposterous undertaking. The last thing he needed was Elise Conway.

But it was not to be so.

Although Adam responded only in a series of monosyllabic grunts and nods, Elsie managed to carry on a breathless soliloquy discussing her recent travels. The weather, the flight, the food, her health, Adam's health, Adam's sex appeal, and even a random tidbit she'd heard about a newly discovered mummy. When she finally came up for air, Adam was almost dizzy with the amount of useless trivia rocketing about in his brain.

"So what about you, Adam? What was the most exciting thing you did on your trip?"

He looked her straight in the eyes and decided to go for broke.

"I touched a dead man's penis."

Thus ended the brief in-flight affair between Elsie Conway and Adam Barfield.

As Elsie quickly busied herself in a romance novel, Adam alternately napped, ate tasteless meals, and made vague plans about his immediate future, until at last below them lay the sparkling waters of San Francisco Bay.

Adam was moved, as always, by the beauty of the landing, but he wasted no time in shouldering his carry-ons and making his way to the baggage carousel. After a speedy trip through customs, he caught the 3B bus to the BART station, a series of trains running through the Bay Area that took Adam almost all the way to his door in Berkeley.

The four walls of his home had a comforting, soothing effect after his long absence, but Adam knew sleep was an impossibility. The sense of order and belonging restored his focus and gave him a clarity of thought that had eluded him on the plane. He paced around his spacious apartment and scribbled random thoughts on a notepad. Now that he'd ventured down this road, the task ahead of him seemed endless, and he didn't want to waste any time getting started.

A quick call to the lab verified that the FedEx package had arrived and was properly stored in the tissue bank. A quick call to the dean clarified his schedule for the next few weeks and welcomed him back. A quick call to his senile housekeeper told him why all his indoor plants had died.

With nothing left to do but wheedle away the hours until he could get into the lab, Adam took a shower and fell into a restless sleep, drifting in and out of mummies and withered philodendrons.

By the next morning Adam was a powder keg of energy. He flew through his morning routine and made it out the door with twenty minutes to spare. Stopping only to grab a coffee and bagel, he headed directly for the lab.

Three graduate students were already hunched over their research projects when Adam swept into the room. They glanced up with smiles and the standard salutations, tapping their pencils distractedly as they asked after his sabbatical. This was why Adam loved grad students; they were like him. Socially awkward, sure, but adept in the questions that lay waiting to be resolved beneath their ready fingertips. He greeted each by name and got a brief update on the development of their work. A lengthier consult would be required, an office interview and a written report, but for now he left them to their own devices and hurried to the tissue bank to collect his prize.

There it was, sitting innocuously amongst the other, legitimate samples. Adam retrieved it carefully and situated himself at the cold box with his microscope, extension tools, and a selection of dyes and stains. From now on, the job would be exacting, boring, and tedious. Each section of tube and tissue had to be stripped of the most obscure sperm while maintaining sterile and extremely cold conditions.

As Adam painstakingly dissected each bit of tissue and located the sperm, he longed to pass the mindless task to one of the students. This sort of work was beneath him. But last night he had made the resounding decision that the only way to carry his project to fruition would be to maintain the utmost secrecy. So he hid away with his dyes and microscopes and toiled alone.

After a few hours, Maren Dixon, Adam's favorite TA, stopped by to inspect the work in progress and welcome him back. She asked him the same banal questions as the others, but with a great deal more underlying interest. Maren had always been interested. Adam had divorced many years ago and had dated very few women since finding himself single. Maren was one of the few.

What had started as an agreeable companionship in the lab had developed from dates into overnight stays, although they had somehow never progressed to naked sex. Adam's problem now was that Maren was committed. And Adam was committed to his work.

"Well, I'll let you get back to it." She smiled as she walked back to the door. "But give me a call when you have some free time; we should celebrate your welcome home."

Her eyes swept the lab table, but she didn't ask any questions and Adam didn't volunteer any information. This was the sort of work on which everyone who ever worked in a lab had clocked countless hours. There was nothing unusual to raise her suspicions.

"We'll get together soon," Adam promised.

The lock clicked shut behind her, but Adam stared vacantly at the door for long after she'd gone, his thoughts ranging out in a millions different directions.

He knew he had to make a concrete plan as to what he wanted to do with the potential contained in these tiny spermatozoa. He had definitively crossed the moral divide by invading the corpse and removing the testicles, and now was setting out upon a singularly dangerous road. Now, the future use of the Iceman would be determined by his desires, not the greater good. Or in the long run, would it be the greater good? Regardless, by all scientific and legal standards, any research gleaned from such an infraction would be forever tainted with scandal and disrepute.

For possibly the first time in his life, Adam found the lab too quiet. The little space was rapidly filling with all his unanswered questions and the weight of the implications of what he'd done.

He would need a plan, yes. And in order to make that plan…he would need some coffee.

Chapter 3

Adam sat alone at an outdoor café, sipping an espresso as he planned a future with the purloined sperm. Normally, a crowded bistro wasn't his destination of choice. The boisterous, ever-changing bustle of people was exactly the kind of thing that triggered some of the worst aspects of his Asperger's. The anxiety, the mental retreat. It was for precisely this reason that he'd gravitated towards his particular profession; science relied upon order, detail, and pristine calm.

A baby stroller crashed into the leg of his table, and Adam grabbed at his coffee before it could spill. He glared at the retreating parents, and could have sworn that a tiny finger flipped him off.

Not so much pristine calm out here. Chaos reigned. In fact, contrary to Adam's hopes, the open air was doing nothing to help his scattered thoughts collect themselves. He rubbed his eyes hopelessly and stared down into his cup. This was why he had gone on sabbatical in the first place. A quiet respite to ease his mind and settle his nerves.

Quiet.

The irony was not lost on him, and despite his present condition, he almost had to smile. For God's sake — what had he gotten himself into?

"Adam?"

Adam looked up with a start into the shaded eyes of Kevin McDonale, a fellow professor who'd worked at the university for the last five years. McDonale taught civics, and he and Adam rarely ran into each other, but they had, on occasion, grabbed drinks with some of their other colleagues at a favorite bar across town.

"I thought that was you." He took off his sunglasses and pulled out the chair across from Adam with a smile. "I hardly ever see you out here. Welcome back!"

"Thanks." Adam leaned forward with a returning smile and beckoned for the barista to bring another coffee.

"To go," McDonale instructed her. "I've actually got to get back. I'm filling in today for Helen."

Adam struggled to return his focus to the present. It had been off gallivanting with Neolithic ghosts in the Italian Alps.

"Helen?" he repeated with a slight frown. "Is everything okay?"

"Oh yeah." McDonale took a scalding gulp from his cup. "She and Lydia finally found a donor; they're meeting with the surrogate tonight."

Helen Vance and Lydia Zarlengo might have caused quite the scandal when they came out to the rest of the faculty by getting married, but at a campus that prided itself on forward-thinking, they were supported and accepted with open arms. But the fairytale had stopped there. With Lydia's infertility and Helen's inability to safely carry a child, the new couple despaired of ever having a family. The feverish quest for a donor and surrogate began, and each member of the staff was accustomed to getting little updates. It now appeared that the search had finally paid off.

Adam sipped his coffee, taking a second to process the news. A vague yet decisive "something" clicked into place, and as the caffeine circulated through his body, the first glimmers of a plan began to emerge.

"Anyway, got to run." McDonale grabbed his satchel and clapped Adam on the shoulder as he made his leave. "Good to have you back!"

"Take care, Kevin."

The trip to the café hadn't been a wasted effort after all.

Surrogacy.

If Adam had a wife, and that wife became pregnant...then he would have joint control over the offspring with no intervention from the news, the authorities, or the scientific community at large. But while this could technically be done, it would involve a monstrous deception, devious scheming, an ungodly amount of arrogance, and most importantly, it would include a huge variable as to whether or not his wife would actually conceive the child. But with surrogacy....

The DNA would belong entirely to him; no questions, no arguments, no variables.

Adam grabbed his jacket, threw some money on the table, and hurried back to BART. It was time to talk to someone as clinical, steadfast, and single-minded as himself.

It was time to consult with Google.

Four hours, five coffees, and seven notepads later, Adam's plan was rapidly leaving its infancy.

As it turned out, a new enterprise known as "reproductive outsourcing" was a rapidly expanding business in India. The premise was exactly as the name would suggest. Send your sperm overseas; come back in nine months to collect your baby.

At first Adam was uneasy with the idea of conducting such a critical transaction in a distant country, but the more he studied the Indian program, the more he became convinced. For one thing, the total cost amounted to about twenty-five thousand dollars, roughly a third of what it would be in the United States. That would include all the medical procedures and payment to the surrogate mother, as well as air fare and hotels for two trips to India — one for the fertilization, and a second to collect the baby.

Then there was the custodial exclusivity. The egg donor and surrogate mother would be two different women to prevent bonding with the child. Furthermore, the donor, surrogate, and future parents would never be allowed to meet. According to the Indian Council of Medical Research, all surrogates were required to forego any rights to the children. Their name was not allowed on the birth certificate, and absolute confidentiality was guaranteed.

Profiles of the various women would be sent to Adam for his perusal. He could choose from such criteria as education, employment, physical characteristics, and social status.

It would be as simple as browsing online for the perfect pair of shoes.

Adam frowned as his mind automatically tagged on this last bit. Was he really considering this? Retail hunting for genetics? Shopping for a *baby*?

The empty mugs and notepads went crashing to the floor as he sprang to his feet, running his hands manically through his hair. There must be something wrong with him. Twelve months of mild elevation sickness must have damaged his capacity for rational thought. What else could explain this behavior? Climate change? Food poisoning? Perhaps Mercury was in retrograde.

Adam slid to the floor with his hands over his eyes. He lowered his head beneath his knees, and slowly the world stopped spinning. He was poised on the edge of possibly the greatest scientific discovery of the century. Yes, it was breaking some vital rules, but what historical giant hadn't? Had John Watson minded the red tape when he made a critical breakthrough in the study of classical conditioning? Had Charles Darwin stayed within the societally-structured guidelines when he published his theory of evolution? Galileo was almost killed for suggesting the Earth wasn't the center of the universe.

Some things transcended the laws of society. Some things had precedence. This was one of those things.

Adam took a deep breath, got to his feet, and sat back down in front of his computer. He started contacting surrogacy clinics. The next day he was forwarded a welcoming packet of information, as well as the first batch of donor profiles for his consideration. He scrolled through the pages with a pencil and a frown, determined to facilitate the perfect conditions for his specimen's birth.

The clinics were very thorough. All the donor candidates were under thirty, healthy, well-educated, and already had at least one living child. They had tested negative for every prevalent disease, and had routine scans and examinations at the clinics.

Despite the trove of information, Adam still had significant questions. Would he be listed as the biological parent on the child's birth certificate? What about immigrations laws? Was DNA testing required to confirm the parental relation before he could leave the country? How did they ensure the surrogate followed a proper prenatal regimen?

He sent back an email with a list of these questions before flipping down the screen on his laptop and rubbing his eyes. It was already three in the morning; he'd have to get up in just a few hours to get back to the lab to finish preparing the sperm. Without the sperm, there would be no baby. And without the baby, an entire world of scientific revelation might lay untapped and dormant forever.

Adam would need his sleep. The weight of that world rested on his shoulders now. He must prove ready for it.

The alarm rang much sooner than Adam would have liked, and he dragged himself out of bed and headed straight back down to the coffee maker. At this rate, he need not worry about the scientific ramifications of his study. He would develop a series of stomach ulcers and bleed out long before that was an issue.

As the machine hummed and hissed its way to life, Adam checked his email. There was a response from one of his top choice clinics in India, as well as another list of donors. They had provided a clear and succinct list of answers to his questions, as well as offering to schedule an online consult to go into greater detail. Adam appreciated the efficiency, and as he took his first sips of the brew, he settled himself down to read.

The clinic promised an easy transition facilitated by a medically-oriented team of lawyers that was in place to handle all the legal aspects relating to the surrogacy, custodianship, and immigration. The International DNA lab tested the parents as well as the babies, and genetic testing of the infant could be performed using cord blood. Making a mental note to decline these particular services, Adam read on. The surrogate's continuing health was monitored carefully by the clinic, and he would receive frequent updates as to her condition. He would also get multiple updates as to the exact delivery date so he could arrange for timely passage to India.

We will let you know in plenty of time for you to arrange to travel to India and receive your precious gift....

More precious than they knew. By every modern standard, this child would be a miracle. A fact which made selecting the egg donor all the more critical.

Adam gathered up the profiles and threw them in his briefcase before heading to the lab. Maren was already there, along with the other grad students, and she followed him back to the cold box as he took off his coat and set down his things.

He hardly noticed her standing there as he considered the task before him. What qualities would he want in the baby's mother? Would aesthetics be important? Not from a scientific standpoint. Although he would want the child to have light enough skin to pass for his own....

"...expecting you to call."

Adam looked up and realized Maren had been talking the entire time. He stared at her appraisingly for a moment, considering her stature and features with an almost critical gaze.

"Maren, what qualities would you look for in a woman?"

She blinked. "Maybe we're not on the same page...."

Adam froze for a moment before catching himself and forcing a chuckle. "No, I mean, scientifically speaking. Genetically. What characteristics do you think make for the strongest offspring?"

"You're building a sex-robot, aren't you?"

Adam's mouth fell open. "What?"

Maren laughed and flung her hair back over her shoulder. "We were all speculating." She gestured outside to where the other students were hard at work. "As to what the great professor could be doing, locked away in the cold all by himself."

This time it was Adam's turn to laugh. Sometimes he forgot how young Maren and the rest of them were. Living in the lab, it was easy to lose perspective.

"And who guessed robot?"

Maren perched on the edge of the table. "Tim. I voted for a simpler, Jekyll-and-Hyde-type experiment."

"You caught me." Adam held up his hands. "And soon you'll all beg for your lives."

She grinned but paused, waiting for some sort of explanation. Adam glanced around quickly, concocting the first of what would surely be many lies.

"A friend of mine, uh, asked my help in selecting an egg donor for a surrogate. She...."

"Oh, Ms. Vance?"

Adam stared at Maren like she'd thrown him a life-raft. "Yes." He smiled. "Ms. Vance."

He couldn't have asked for better timing to his colleague's happy news.

"I'm having trouble figuring out what attributes...I mean to say, what genetic characteristics would make for the best choice."

Maren hopped off the table, and all at once she was standing right in front of him.

"Well, it all depends on what you want in a woman."

Adam caught his breath but remembered his objective. If Maren wanted to talk this way, he'd certainly play along. As long as what she said continued to be relevant.

"I'd want a smart woman," he began, with a somewhat resigned awareness that whatever he said, Maren would apply to herself. "Intelligence is key."

"With a wicked sense of humor?"

"Humor is irrelevant," Adam replied briskly.

Maren took a step back, her expression shifting with the change in his tone. "Appearance?"

Adam considered. "Relative...but not critical."

"Immune system." Adam raised his eyebrows and she shrugged. "Well if you're truly going for the 'strongest possible offspring,' I'd look into medical history, not just their current health."

"Yes," Adam murmured, scribbling something down, "any degenerative illness could be a catastrophe...." He settled back in his chair and turned away from her, focused on his work.

Maren backed slowly to the door. "Well, it looks like you don't need me here. You've got everything under control."

Adam didn't look up from his writing. "Yes. Thanks Maren, you've been a big help."

The door pulled shut and Adam spread out the candidate profiles on the table before him. Sure enough, each one listed an intensive medical family history. He poured through each one in painstaking detail, seeing every ear infection as a disaster, every fever as a calamity. Once all the possible deterrents had been eliminated, he was left with only a select few.

In the end, he left it to chance. He flipped a coin and thus selected a lighter-skinned, amber-eyed donor from northern India; one who demonstrated high intelligence and had a tall, lithe body.

"Goodnight, Professor."

Adam looked up in surprise to see the grad students filing out. The sky was already dark, and the lights were off in most of the other buildings. Maren was already gone.

"Goodnight, Nicholas," he replied, scooping his papers into his bag and returning the tissue sample to its container.

By the time he made it back to his house it was coming up on eleven, and Adam abruptly realized he was starving. He flipped through the take-out menus stuck to his refrigerator, and in honor of his decision he decided to order Indian.

The stage was set, and all the players were in position. All Adam had to do now was FedEx his treasured frozen sperm to the clinic and wait for the good news.

It was at this point that Adam hesitated, looking around the barren walls of his apartment. After this, there would be no going back. There would be no more quiet, no more calm. He would be bringing a living, breathing, talking creature into this house. It would live with him. It would have a room next to his. For the next eighteen years.

To be honest, Adam wasn't worried about bonding with the child. He had never taken to children, and truly believed that were it not for this remarkable set of circumstances, he would happily carry out the rest of his days as a bachelor. In fact, as he had made his furtive plans, Adam realized that he was hardly thinking of the fertilization as a child at all.

It would be an experiment, nothing more. He would keep it secret, and study it within an environment he could control.

And the world would reap the benefits.

There was a knock on the door. "Did somebody order Indian?"

Chapter 4

Of the five eggs procured from the donor, all five progressed to the number of cell divisions required for implantation. On the fifth day of this procedure, the blastocyst with the most potential was placed in the surrogate's womb.

Adam was so agitated during this interval that he seldom slept or ate. He called in sick to the university and spent most of his time pacing in his apartment. What if the embryo didn't take? What if all this scheming and worry had been for nothing? He had so convinced himself that the operation was a doomed failure that he hardly believed it when he got a sudden phone call.

"Hello, is this Dr. Barfield?"

The international connection was rough, and Adam struggled to make out the words. "Yes?"

"Dr. Barfield, we wanted to let you know as soon as possible that the surrogate implanted with the donor egg you selected from our profiles took a blood test this morning."

Adam held his breath, clutching the phone in his fist. "And?"

"Congratulations, sir. She is pregnant."

There was a slight pause.

"Dr. Barfield?"

Adam sat down at the kitchen table, head in his hands. "Yes, I heard you. Thank you for the call." He hung up the phone and stared out the window at the setting California sun.

A woman halfway around the world was now carrying his child. *Otzi's* child.

The next few months were a blur. At times it was almost as if the pregnancy wasn't happening. Adam's life continued on as it had always done. He got up, grabbed a coffee, and went to the lab. He even took Maren out to dinner a few times. But no one in the world, besides a handful of doctors and two women in India, knew that he was soon to have a child. There were times when he almost forgot it himself.

But then, at twenty-three weeks, the ultrasound arrived.

Adam stared at the lumpy patchwork of black and white. It almost resembled a Rorschach test. If he cocked his head to the side, it looked like a lopsided bird. But perhaps more importantly, it was a boy.

This was a good thing, Adam decided. Now the child could be directly and more accurately compared to his father. His *real* father, that was. Not for the first time, Adam wondered absently at how Otzi would react if he knew that five-thousand years after his death, he would produce a son.

Holding the thin picture in his hand, Adam lingered in the kitchen. Should he put it on the refrigerator? Wasn't that what people did? He pushed aside some of the takeout menus and held it up appraisingly. Then his face hardened and he took it down.

No. It would go in his office. The first piece of tangible evidence for study.

After locking it securely in his desk, Adam wandered back to the living room and looked about with pride. Everything was going according to plan. His revolutionary experiment was almost ready, and in just a few short months, he would have an actual child.

Then he looked around the room again, this time in absolute horror.

In just a few short months...he would have an actual child.

He'd never realized how sharp the edges of his furniture were. In fact, everything in the room was sharp or could be easily swallowed. He kicked the edge of his coffee table in dismay. He was living in a virtual death trap.

In a fit of nerves, he got online and was about to order a suede living room set before he checked himself. It wasn't just the baby-proofing; he would need help caring for the child itself, especially in its infancy. He had never been around infants or children, and was particularly unsuited for the job. This would be no ordinary child, and he would need to optimum care in order to promote its healthy development.

The old-fashioned idea of a wet nurse appealed to him...a young woman provide to stay with the infant for the first year or two. Moreover, he thought he was in a good place to procure one. There was an abortion clinic nearby, with students of all ages terminating pregnancies at all stages. All he needed to do was to find a young woman who was producing milk and would be willing to feed and care for the infant. In return, he would be able to provide a home, as well as tuition and a salary.

The next day he went to the clinic and talked to the director, explaining his surrogacy situation in India and describing the characteristics he sought in the young woman he'd like to hire. To his extreme relief, the director told him that this sort of request was not at all uncommon, and he would be in contact in the next few days with any potential candidates.

Who the director came up with was Kendra, a sweet and tender young girl, glad for a place to live and the prospect of paid tuition and salary. She was determined to complete her education, and had refused to allow an unplanned pregnancy to deter her from getting her diploma. And while Kendra recognized this as an admittedly strange situation, it was a direct path to that goal.

Having secured a nurse, Adam turned his attention to finding a nanny, someone to provide care until the boy was of school age. This time, he sought help through the university.

Lilly was a dream come true. She immediately caught Adam's eye, in more ways than one, and he hastened to do whatever was necessary to secure her. Not only did she appear to delight in infants and children, but she was a student majoring in early childhood education and development. In many ways the child would serve as a case study for her as well, and perhaps one day, the subject for her thesis.

Lilly wouldn't need a room as she would only be at the house during the day, so that just left Adam to furnish one for Kendra and another for the baby. Cribs, car seats, strollers, toys…these went side by side in Adam's shopping cart with stopwatches, measuring tape, a video camera, tape recorders, and enough stationary to paper his way across the Atlantic. In addition to these inconspicuous study tools, Adam discreetly pocketed a syringe and took it home from the lab.

After all, the baby had been created for a solitary purpose — DNA.

He could have all the toys he wanted, as long as Adam had regular blood samples for study.

The California Office of Vital Records had agreed to list Adam as father on the birth certificate, which required that the Superior Court name the intended parent as the legal parent. Because the certificate had to be registered with the Office of Vital Records within ten days of the birth, the judgment would to be presented to the birth records agency shortly after. Adam made sure to secure the judgment early enough in the surrogate's pregnancy that when the time of delivery drew near, his name was on all the proper documents.

A logistical quagmire, but it would cover a multitude of sins.

Finally, with all the technicalities squared away, there was only one thing left to do. But as simple as it had sounded on paper, it suddenly seemed like the hardest task yet.

One that Adam was not looking forward to....

***

Maren's eyes widened for a moment as she regarded the professor. She'd learned over the course of their time together not to be surprised by things. His mental peculiarities had always rendered him what others politely referred to as "odd." But Maren knew better. Adam was a force to be reckoned with. His unnatural focus and almost unsettling proclivity for details had created the perfect scientist. He was committed to his work. Dedicated to his lab.

That's why this sudden yearning for a child made no sense to her.

"I don't understand," she said again. "You're going to have a baby?"

Adam nodded patiently. "Through a surrogate with a separate egg donor in India. I have an open ticket to fly out there and pick him up...I'm just waiting for the call."

Him? This mystery-child was a boy?

The unfaltering predictability of Maren's life suddenly shattered as she stared at the man before her. When he'd called and insisted they meet, she'd assumed it would be for a dinner, or perhaps even an overnight rendezvous. She was wearing her special underwear....

"This has been going on for months?" she asked flatly. "The whole time we've been dating."

"That's how pregnancy works, Maren."

Maren missed the humor.

So this was why he'd been acting so differently, so cagey in the lab. Going off by himself for hours at a time and disregarding their usual partnership. Perhaps she'd been too casual, not been insistent enough? After all, they hadn't even had sex, and here he wanted a family!

She lowered her voice as a wave of sadness washed over her. "I see. Well Adam, I wish you all the best of luck—"

"I was hoping...." He cut her off. "I was hoping that when we get back, maybe you would come over and meet him?"

Maren frowned. For a moment a distant future flashed before her eyes, one she had long ago forbidden herself from considering. The brilliant scientist with Maren at his side. A lovely home in the Berkeley Hills. And a beautiful child to complete the picture.

Her eyes misted over and she hastened to focus on the professor, who it seemed was just as intently focusing on her.

For the first time Adam saw in Maren all the potential usefulness she had so forcefully advertised when lobbying for the position of his TA. This was an intelligent woman, yes, but she could be nurturing as well. Just because he had never considered taking their relationship to the next level didn't mean he was blind to her ambitions. Perhaps there was a way to solve two problems in one fell swoop.

Maren kissed him at the door on his way out. Then they turned in separate directions, both feeling very pleased with the unspoken implications that had just transpired. Both feeling as though they had the upper hand.

Adam was hardly through his own door when Kendra ran through the kitchen, clutching her cell phone in her hand.

"It's time!" she trilled, waving the phone around in excitement. "They said she just went into labor; I was about to call you!"

Adam blinked, taking a second to adjust to how very quickly his world was turning. This morning, his only priority had been to try to stop his girlfriend from leaving him. Now he was on the brink of a serious relationship and was about to fly halfway around the world to pick up his child. He thought briefly of the ultrasound picture in his study.

"Then we have to go!" He sprang into action, heading nowhere in particular. "Do you have your things? You have your passport and your bag, correct?"

Kendra giggled. "Yes, *Dad*. And yours are already in the car. Let's go get the little guy!"

Two hours later they were on the plane. The clinic was located in Delhi, which was a flight of a little over twenty-two hours. By all accounts, Kendra was more excited than Adam. She had never ventured outside the U.S. and planes were still a bit of a novelty to her. Adam tolerated her as best he could as she gawked out the window and gushed about how she couldn't wait to hold the baby. They were, quite simply, in two different worlds.

Adam was requiring perfection. Ten fingers. Ten toes. And a living sample of DNA so incomprehensible that it would shake the scientific community to its core. If the baby was green and had two heads, Kendra would most likely still be calling him her "little cuddle bug."

They finally touched down at India Gandhi International Airport, and after the interminable customs delay, they caught an Easy Cab.

"Where to?" the driver asked in surprisingly proficient English. Kendra and Adam spoke at the same time.

"The hospital!"

"The InterContin—the hospital!"

Adam had hoped that they could head to the hotel. The hospital had instructions to call as soon as the baby was born; they didn't need to be there when it was happening. But it would certainly appear, especially in the presence of Kendra, that a sufficient amount of enthusiasm was required.

The car was sweltering and they immediately rolled down their windows, only to be engulfed in a torrent of hot, dry wind. The driver told them that this was the "loo." It had been the subject of many poems and Indian works of fiction. "The trees lose their flowers. Their leaves fall. Their bare branches stretch up to the sky begging for water…."

Kendra hung on every word, absolutely entranced, while Adam texted on his Blackberry.

For all his lyrical limitations, the driver knew the city well, and before long, they pulled into the hospital's emergency loading bay. They had no sooner located the nurses' station before they were told that a healthy, six pound baby boy had been delivered just a few hours earlier.

Kendra burst into instant tears as the lead nurse asked Adam, "Are you the father?"

Adam flashed a quick smile. "That's what's on the papers."

It seemed too easy to create a life from deception and lies.

The nurse smiled warmly. "Well then, let's go meet your son."

As they climbed into the elevator and rode it to the correct floor, Adam suddenly found himself increasingly nervous. Despite his lack of genetic contribution, he was still directly responsible for the birth of this child. It was a life created solely from his whimsy and recklessness, and now that he was about to see it in person, he was anxious as to how he would react. These sorts of deeply emotional upheavals were big red flags with Asperger's. Between that and his preexisting apathy towards children in general, Adam braced himself as he entered the room.

But he needn't have bothered. For there was nothing less threatening in the world than the little baby sleeping under his blanket.

Kendra stopped with her hands over her mouth as Adam ventured a step closer. He'd wanted perfection, and the baby was perfect. A perfect fusion of past and present. A flawless specimen sleeping soundly as he sucked his thumb.

Almost absentmindedly, he stroked the baby's foot. Kendra's eyes welled up at the parental display as Adam's eyes zeroed in on the heel. This was the best spot to take blood so as to avoid any identifying marks or bruising.

"We just need you to finish up some paperwork, Dr. Barfield, and then you're all ready to take him home."

Adam nodded silently, as entranced by the little one as the women. He held his breath as he approached the incubator, staring down at the tiny face and miniscule fingers.

"Let's get you home."

He rubbed the baby's heel again and murmured so softly, Kendra didn't hear him.

"We have a lot of work to do."

Chapter 5

Adam sipped slowly at his orange juice, watching Kendra nurse the baby before they both fell into an exhausted sleep. Every stewardess on the plane had stopped by at least twice to check on the little infant, and while Adam found their intrusions annoying, it did distract both Kendra and the newborn long enough to give him some time to think.

He would have to give the baby a name. Something distinctive, as befitting his unique scientific and historical standing, yet innocuous enough for him to be called on the day to day. At first he had considered the name Adam. Although not a religious man, there was something appropriate in naming the child after the "first man." Not only that, but friends and colleagues would find nothing at all unusual with Adam following the societal tradition of naming his child after himself. But the more he thought about it, the less he liked the idea. This baby was not a religious wonder, he was a scientific one. He would be a champion of genetics, not Christ.

After a few hours of thoughtful deliberation, Adam decided to mix the two. He would call the baby "Gene." A fusion of Genesis, the first book in the Bible, and the very namesake of the genetic world that he was about to overturn.

If a middle name was needed, it would be Adam.

Satisfied, he leaned back and pulled out his notepad, jotting down ideas as he considered the logistics. He had told his associates and friends that he had longed for a child and had hired a surrogate in India. Although puzzled, they had proven most supportive, and no further explanation seemed to be required. He had no immediate family in the area to speak of, and Maren had already been informed. That left the matter of the child itself.

The nature of the project was rooted in secrecy, so the files and tests would be coded and kept secret to everyone except Adam himself. And as for the tests themselves…?

Adam smiled to himself as *The Resurrected* came on as the in-flight movie. For the next two hours, he watched the actors toil away with cloning and genetic experimentation. Although the movie was technically considered to be science-fiction, his own experiments would run along the same lines. He was especially interested in the functioning of the baby's immune system, as well as his learning capabilities. He would keep a detailed diary, an on-going anthropological case study of the boy, whilst collecting regular blood samples from his heel.

The secrecy required would be oppressive, but if word of this child leaked out the results would be devastating, both from the press and from the scientific community. And the consequences of what he had done from an ethical standpoint were disastrous. He would be blacklisted, if not charged criminally. Secrecy was key.

He was building a delicate house of cards. If he succeeded, the world would be at his fingertips. But one wrong move, and the entire thing would come crashing down and bury him underneath.

"More orange juice, sir?"

Adam smiled. "Please."

When the plane finally touched down in San Francisco, Adam and Kendra were more haggard and tired than they had been at any point on their outgoing journey. Little Gene had demanded many feedings and changes, and was apt to cry if not tended to immediately. The wait through customs was comparable to purgatory itself, and words could not express their relief when they were finally able to pile into a cab and head back to Berkeley.

Adam looked wistfully out the window as his BART station grew smaller and smaller in the distance. Gone were his days of mobile freedom. There would be no more hopping on the bus or Metro with this entourage.

The first order of business when they got home was sleep. Even Gene seemed to understand the importance of this, and he kept his hungry interruptions to a minimum. The next day, Adam made a trip to the grocery store to restock the kitchen. When he returned, he gave Kendra some well-deserved free time, ordered a large pizza, and pulled out some wine.

There was someone Gene needed to meet.

"Oh my goodness, Adam! He's beautiful!"

Maren picked Gene up gently in her arms and cradled him against her face. Despite being finicky about some things, the baby had no problem with new people and lost no time in wrapping his little hands throughout her long hair.

"He's quite something," Adam agreed, pouring himself a second glass.

Maren grinned and detangled Gene's tiny fingers. "Who's his pediatrician?"

Adam hit himself in the head. He'd spent a good thirty minutes in the toy train aisle, debating which model would stimulate the most brain growth, but he'd completely forgotten to arrange a doctor for the child.

"Don't worry." Maren smiled, nuzzling Gene's warm little neck. "I have a couple of names. I'll schedule an appointment for you."

Adam leaned back in his chair and surveyed her appreciatively. "Thanks, Maren."

"No problem." Gene put a chubby hand on her cheek and she glowed. "After all, this little guy and I are going to have to get to know each other." She glanced up with deliberate nonchalance. "If I'm going to be in his life."

Maren watched over the lab for the next couple of days as Adam got acclimated with the baby and Kendra. And at the end of the week, with no little amount of anxiety, Adam loaded Gene into the car seat and took him to his first official doctor's appointment.

The waiting room looked like something out of a Stephen King novel. The range of carnage wreaked by such little creatures seemed impossible. Everywhere Adam looked were children screaming, fathers looking bored, and mothers trying to hold it together while verging on tears.

He settled with Gene in the farthest corner away from everyone and tilted his lap so that the baby was facing his direction. He didn't want the kid to get any ideas.

The longer he waited the more anxious he became. What if the doctor noticed something different? Something Adam hadn't thought to hide? What if he had one of those posters on his wall showing the stages of evolution, and when he held Gene up in front of it, he shook his head and said, "No, that isn't right."

A building block went sailing an inch from Adam's head and he pulled Gene a little closer. On second thought, his baby looked to be the most evolved one here. He leaned forward, looking deep into the child's ocean-blue eyes.

"Just...be yourself," he found himself whispering.

"Dr. Barfield?"

Adam jumped and got to his feet. "That's me." He flashed a tight smile to the nurse. "Just doing a little pre-game huddle, you know?"

She smiled politely. "The doctor will see you now."

They followed her into a back room and sat down for only a few seconds before the doctor came rushing through the door.

"Sorry for the wait, I'm Doctor Levinson."

He extended his hand and Adam shifted Gene so he could take it.

"No problem. It's a bit of a mad house out there."

The doctor's eyes never left his clipboard. "Not really." When he glanced up at Adam's look of confusion, he smiled. "This is your first child, isn't it?"

Adam flushed. "Yes, this is Gene."

He held the baby forward and Dr. Levinson set him squarely in the middle of the exam table.

"It certainly is!" He beamed at Gene, simultaneously flashing a light in his eyes to check for pupillary responses. "Well, let's take a look at you."

With skilled hands, he stood Gene up and took him through the usual courses, pausing every now and again to write something down on his clipboard. Adam strained covertly in his chair, but was unable to make out what it said.

"Have you been doing this long?" he asked, trying to mask his efforts as he leaned around behind the doctor.

Come to think of it, the man did look awfully young. Too young to be entrusted with children. Too young to be in charge of the clipboard.

"Five years," Levinson replied, shifting forward to write something else.

"Five years." Adam walked casually around to the other side on the pretext of comforting Gene, when the doctor went suddenly to the counter, taking his chart with him.

Adam raged in silent frustration and regarded his nemesis. He needed those notes. Every bit of information at this stage was important.

"And where was it that you got your diploma?" he asked testily. What hack school would let this guy in?

Levinson returned with a small tape measure and began calculating the circumference of Gene's head. "That would be Princeton."

Princeton. The school for those who couldn't get into Harvard.

Only vaguely aware that he was redirecting his nerves into randomly assigned anger, Adam couldn't resist a small scoff.

Levinson turned around. "You teach at the university here, don't you? Maren said you were a professor."

The casual way in which he referred to Maren made Adam dislike him all the more.

"Yes. For *nine* years."

The doctor smiled. "Well, Maren seems to think very highly of you."

"How is my *son*?"

The clipboard came up between them.

"Your son...is developing exactly like a baby should. He's alert and responsive. High average in both height and weight percentiles, as well as head circumference. All in all, a very healthy little boy."

Adam breathed a silent sigh of relief while Levinson retrieved a syringe from the counter.

"I'm going to give him his first hepatitis shot, but the rest of the standard immunizations won't start until he's about two months old."

"That's fine," Adam replied, and he found himself smiling at Gene over the doctor's shoulder.

The women were right; he was a beautiful baby. He had very dark hair that covered almost all of his head, but was developing a little bald spot which Adam subconsciously compared to his own thinning locks. It was still too early to determine whether his eyes would be blue or brown, and his skin was a light yet dusky cream.

"Well, we're all finished." Levinson straightened up and put the cap on his pen.

Adam picked up Gene and headed towards the door. "Do you think...is it possible for me to get a copy of the chart?" he asked. "For my own peace of mind."

"I'm afraid that wouldn't be allowed, but if you shoot me an email, I'll be sure to forward along any important information."

He handed Adam his card before showing them out the door and getting to his next patient.

Daniel Levinson, M.D.

Adam glanced at Gene, unimpressed. Levinson was a deceptively old sounding name. Adam supposed this was how the doctor got the bulk of his clientele.

"How did it go?" Kendra asked when Gene and Adam arrived home.

Adam took off his coat and threw the crumpled business card into the trash. "Fine. He said Gene is perfectly average."

"Well, that's not true!" Kendra rushed forward and took the baby from Adam's arms, cooing and using that baby-voice that Adam found detestable. "He's amazing!"

"Yes." For once he agreed with her. "He certainly is."

He did it that night, sneaking in while the baby was sleeping. With hands far more capable than those of Daniel Levinson, he pulled the cap off the syringe and pressed it gently into the infant's heel. Gene stirred softly, but did not awaken. Adam watched with strange focus as the tiny capsule filled with blood. Then, as quietly as he'd come in, Adam slipped out into the hall.

The light flashed on.

"What are you doing?"

Adam jumped a mile and narrowly avoided crushing the glass vial in his pocket. Kendra was blinking back at him, eyes adjusting to the bright light.

"I thought I heard him wake," Adam gasped, willing himself to be calm. "You should keep a better eye on him."

Kendra glanced at once into the nursery. "I will," she promised hastily. "I was just coming to check on him."

"Good." Adam slipped backwards towards his study. "Goodnight, Kendra."

"Goodnight."

She vanished into the darkness as Adam locked the door quietly to his study. Flicking on the lamp on the desk, he pulled out some blank slides and his microscope.

So the experiment began....

Chapter 6

There was *so much* to do!

Adam had been studying Gene's blood for the last few months now, and he was nowhere close to being able to identify, let alone understand, all its unique and elusive properties. He spent long hours at the lab, poring over data, only to come home to a screaming baby and a tired wet nurse. Maren helped out when she could, but when she and Adam made plans together, it was usually not to babysit.

So life settled into an exhausting routine. They were easing into the fall semester when Kendra would go to class and Lilly would come to work as a nanny. Adam took care to keep a workable distance between himself and the beautiful coed, holing himself up in his study. There had already been sideways glances, playful lingering at the end of her shift. But Adam was just getting used to having regular sex again, and he had never been less inclined to take any unnecessary risks. Right now, the Barfield house was balanced on a delicate scale. If he strayed too far from the center, the whole thing might capsize.

It was on one of these occasions when Adam heard a car door slam from his study. There was the sound of muffled voices and Lilly called, "Adam? Maren's here to watch Gene. I'm going out for a bit."

Adam leaned back in his chair. "Thanks, Lilly. Have fun."

The house was starting to look a bit like a harem. Different women coming in and out at all hours. What must the neighbors think?

A few seconds later he heard Maren greeting Gene, and he set down his papers and rubbed his eyes. Although he had grown increasingly affectionate towards Maren, and had even developed a decided fondness towards the child, his priority was his work...these papers he was endlessly putting aside to deal with the newfound chaos of his life. With a reluctant sigh, he powered off his computer and joined the rest of them in the living room.

The house was hot and smelled of faintly of cookies, and Adam paused a moment in the doorway, taking it all in.

Gene could sit up now, and could gurgle and coo. He was becoming his own little person, charming, and with a definite personality. He was surprisingly intelligent for a boy of his age, and seemed to be progressing at an accelerated rate. As Adam watched, he wondered which specific genes had accounted for this advanced progression. If only he could get a little peace and quiet, perhaps he could find out.

"What are you doing?"

Adam jumped back to the present. Gene was absorbed with some toy on the ground and Maren was staring at Adam with a strange attentiveness. He was quick to catch himself.

"Just watching the two of you." He smiled easily. "It's nice to see you play together."

Maren seemed to accept this and smiled thoughtfully before straightening up and looking at him head on. It was at this point that Adam realized Maren did not intend to stay. She was still wearing her coat and boots, and her purse hung ready on her shoulder.

"Adam, can we sit down and talk for a minute?"

A rush of adrenaline raised the hair on the back of his neck. Warning. Something was coming.

"Sure," he said mildly, taking a seat.

There was a subtle shift in dynamic, and all at once the tables had turned. He was the student, and she was the professor. He was out of his element, and she was firmly in control.

"Adam...." She turned to face him. "What do you want...for us? What do you see happening?"

Adam considered this for a moment, trying to be as honest as he could. "I would want a healthy, productive relationship. One that benefits us both."

Maren stifled a smile. Typical Adam response. However, in this regard, their interests were one-hundred percent aligned.

"Then marry me."

This time, it was Adam who stifled a smile.

"Did you just propose to me?"

Maren got up with a rather business-like tone. "Well Adam, one of us had to do it."

He blinked at her in utter amazement, and she grinned to herself as she straightened her coat and made her way to the door.

"Watch the baby, Adam; he's about to fall."

Adam whirled around to where Gene had perched on the edge of the coffee table, peering perilously over the edge.

He scrambled to put him safely on the ground, and by the time he looked back around, Maren was gone.

What...just happened?

Adam was still in shock the next day as he settled in to work at the lab. Maren hadn't exactly demanded a response, but it was clear that the ball was in Adam's court. However he acted at their next encounter would set the tone for the rest of their relationship. And if Maren had her way, it would set the tone for the rest of their lives.

Not that he was completely opposed to the idea. As they had discussed many times before, the girls wouldn't be around to help them forever, and the time was fast approaching when Gene would need a mother. Adam needed stability in the house, and to put it frankly, someone to pick up the emotional slack when it came to the child. The more he thought about it, the more the idea made sense. But...*marriage*? Hadn't he already been down that road?

"Professor?"

Adam started. "Yes—Katie? Sorry, I didn't see you there."

The tiny Korean girl smiled. "No problem. I was just asking what kind of sandwich you'd like for lunch. The rest of us are going to pick some up."

"Oh—anything is fine," he replied quickly, glancing in dismay at the fast-moving clock. "Thank you, Katie."

She disappeared with a nod and Adam mentally berated himself as he got back to work. These quiet hours in the lab were becoming increasingly precious and hard to come by. And with the enormity of the task that lay ahead of him, he was in no position to waste them. He put his home troubles aside and returned to his notes.

Gene seemed to possess a super immune system with an inborn immunity to every virus and bacteria that Adam matched it up against. From a scientific standpoint he knew these findings had far-reaching implications, and at present he was trying to replicate the unique immune factors present in the child's blood. So potent were these antibodies that Adam was hopeful, with the right bit of genetic manipulation, he could begin to produce the likes of anti-cancer, anti-AIDS, and anti-Alzheimer's drugs. Anything that enhanced the body's natural immune system.

The sky was the limit, but time was the factor. Projects like this had countless teams of scientists and lab technicians working round the clock to document every slightest detail. Adam couldn't even tell Maren. It was a massive undertaking to be shouldering alone, and throughout the last few months, Adam had caught himself many times wondering if it could even be done.

In many ways, it was a nightmarish Catch-22. Even if he came up with a patent, he couldn't publish it without documentation. He couldn't provide documentation because, for all intents and purposes, Gene, as Otzi's son, did not exist. And if Adam were ever to admit to his indiscretion for the sake of his work, he would most likely go to prison.

"Oh, what a tangled web we weave when first we practice to deceive."

The clock ticked relentlessly onwards and Adam put these despairing thoughts from his head. Regardless of whatever uncertainties lay ahead, research this invaluable couldn't be put to waste. He would move forward.

What Adam needed now were human test subjects. Actual living, breathing people on whom to test his theories. Mixing Gene's blood with the bacteria was one thing, but he couldn't have any conclusive proof until he'd seen what the antibodies would do in a live subject. But you couldn't just go out and find living test subjects without devising and getting approval from the National Institutes of Health. No one would sign up for a lone case study with no official backing. Even those in the end stages of their illness would not be permitted to begin such a course of treatment. And after the appalling Tuskegee syphilis experiment in 1972, where several hundred men were infected and without their knowledge left purposefully untreated, the National Research Act protected the rights of study participants and demanded informed consent.

"Here you go, Professor; we got you turkey and Swiss." Katie muffled a cough in her arm and held out a sandwich. Adam hesitated a moment before taking it.

"Doesn't inspire much appetite," he joked. "You should stop by the student health center before you go home today."

"Already on it." She sniffed wearily. "Anyway — enjoy."

Deciding not to risk it, Adam threw the sandwich in the trash and turned instead to his computer. He spent the next few hours poring over case after experimental case, all of which boiled down to the issue of informed consent. In order to perform scientific testing on a human, you must have the cognizant approval of such human. There seemed to be no way around it.

Adam grabbed a slice of cold pizza and chewed thoughtfully as he packed up his things and headed out through the student lab. Yes, you couldn't experiment on a human. He paused beside Katie's table, where she'd forgotten her woolen sweater hanging on the chair.

But why not experiment on the experiment itself?

He picked up the sweater and twisted the fabric gently between his fingers. Then, without another moment's pause, he stuffed it into his briefcase and headed to the BART.

As he walked up the sidewalk to his house, he saw Maren's car sitting in the drive. With a frustrated grimace, he stopped where he stood.

Of course. His life-altering decision. He'd forgotten.

He heard a chorus of laughter coming from inside as all three women congratulated Gene on some new precedent he'd set for himself. Adam could almost picture them, smiling and cheering, with Gene sitting there in the middle. The venerated child.

All at once, Adam's priorities were clear. Everything he did now would be for the sake of the science. For the sake of the child. In this case, they were one and the same.

Gene would need a mother.

Adam took a breath and walked up the drive. He opened the door to see the three women playing with the wonder-child just as he'd imagined. Maren caught his eye from across the room, and with a movement so slight it might not have happened, he nodded. She beamed in response, and Adam felt a door in his life close forever. But when he looked at Gene, he suddenly saw another one open.

Too much at stake to back out now.

So he took off his coat, put on a smile, and joined them in the living room.

That night, Adam volunteered to put the baby to sleep. Maren was waiting in his own bed, so he'd promised to be quick. He said not a word as he went through the routine motions of pricking the child's heel and pocketing the vial of blood. Gene started to cry and fuss, but Adam was ready with a stuffed giraffe he'd seen Kendra use to calm him.

Once he'd settled down, Adam lifted him gently out of his crib. He rocked him back and forth for a moment, letting him adjust to the rhythm, before reaching down with one hand and grabbing Katie's sweater out of his bag.

He wrapped Gene snuggly inside and settled him back into his little bed.

Time to see what that magic blood of his could really do.

Chapter 7

On the day Adam published his first paper, it took reporters only four hours to find him at the lab. It might have taken them less time than that were they not misled by a loyal colleague.

Broad and potent neutralizing antibodies were isolated from an unknown donor in the Berkeley labs of Adam Barfield. They reveal a New HIV-1 Vaccine Target with the potential to establish immunity....

The press release sounded promising, even to him. He scanned it over coffee as he hid from the flashbulbs and endless barrage of questions waiting just outside. Maren had been calling on the hour, every hour. No doubt she felt some sort of betrayal from having been kept apart from such a revolutionary breakthrough, but he didn't have time to coddle her emotions right now.

He had made the decision to publish in the middle of the night, woken from sleep with this one, solitary desire. There was no immediate requirement that he share the identity of the donor should the donor wish to remain anonymous. For good measure, he'd even crept silently down the hall to where Gene lay asleep in his crib and asked him.

"Do you wish to remain anonymous to the scientific community? Yes? Good."

Informed consent. And Adam, as legal guardian, fully approved.

The decision had come not long after the incident with the sweater. Adam had watched on pins as needles for two days as Katie got sicker and sicker, and Gene remained in perfect health. It appeared as though there was nothing his immune system couldn't overcome. Adam's in vitro tests confirmed this, and it was time the world knew about it.

But reporters were unrelenting, and they continued their siege of the lab. Adam had fended them off with vague statements about the unknown donor; their desire to remain anonymous, and the danger of too much information being leaked before Adam had more proven results. He asked them to respect the donor's right to privacy and focus instead on the amazing opportunities that lay before them.

He should have known it wouldn't have been that simple. There was a louder banging than usual, and Adam glared up at the door.

"Adam, it's Kevin. Let me in!"

The glare faded at once, and Adam hurried through the student lab to open the facility. He locked the door again swiftly as Kevin McDonale rushed inside.

"It's like a circus out there! I thought they were going to claw me to pieces!"

Adam shook his head in dismay. "I had to cancel all my classes. There should be laws against them disrupting the education of students on campus."

McDonale laughed at his friend's bristly exterior. "Well, who can blame them? It's quite the story. All this time we thought you were just being anti-social, but you were in here cooking up the next big thing in genetics!" He lay down on a lab table and stretched out his arms. "I wonder if there's a medal you science guys can win for a thing like this. At any rate, I'm sure the dean will be very proud."

"Yes, he's called." Adam slapped his muddy shoes. "Get your feet off the table."

McDonale sat up. "You could have told me, at least. Your closest friend."

Adam raised his eyebrows. "My closest friend? That I see maybe once a month?"

"Well, I'm going to have to get closer now…now that you're famous."

He burst out laughing and Adam had to join in spite of himself. He took a seat on the adjoining table, and together they listened to the buzzing horde outside.

"I just wish they'd stop with the siege mentality. There's no food in here — I'm starving."

McDonale patted down his jacket pockets. "I have M&M's."

Adam held out his hands. "Gimme."

As he snacked gratefully on his friend's lunch, he thoughtfully considered the crowd.

"They're not even asking the right questions. This is about the science, not the donor. Don't they realize how many people this could help? It doesn't just boil down to one man."

"So the donor's a man…?"

Adam whirled around, but McDonale held up his hands and chuckled.

"I'm only joking. You know, no disrespect, but I really couldn't find genetics any more boring."

"None taken." Adam grinned. "And civics is a real hoot?"

McDonale shrugged. "It is what it is." He hopped down from the table and headed towards the door. "Well, I'm off, now that I've made sure you aren't going all Howard Hughes, filling up bottles with pee and deciding to live in here."

Adam waved the candy above his head. "Thanks, Kevin."

The teacher nodded. "You know, you can tell them the donor is me if you want." He flashed a grin and disappeared into the fray.

Adam's smile faded as the scream of sound filtered in, and he backed once more into the safety of his office.

If only he could take McDonale up on that offer. It might salvage the rest of his sanity.

As it stood, his research was in dire straits. Not only was he in desperate need of more blood, but unless he injected his new vaccine into someone with an actual immune-deficient disease, all this work and study would be for not. He was playing with live ammunition now. He needed a live environment to test it.

He stayed in the lab until almost all the reporters had given up for the day before sneaking out a side door and hurrying along to the catch the train home.

The Berkeley weather had taken on all the aspects of fall, with the low lying fog burning off by noon. The days were brisk and cool, revving up metabolisms and keeping everyone just a little more active. This had been wonderful for Gene in particular, as he tumbled and rolled about, trying to stand up on his own.

By now his care was split by Kendra and Lilly, and Gene seemed to adore them both equally. Kendra's breasts were still beckoning when he saw her, but his nursing was vigorous and brief; he was not a baby that liked to linger, and his attention was always already turned to other things. His hair had gotten a little wave, almost curling, and his eyes were now a deep, dark blue. They were framed by lashes so extravagantly long, they gave his face an appearance close to beauty.

Adam and Maren had finally found their groove. Every night they would have dinner together, pizza and wine, and after, they'd play with Gene until he grew tired and cranky. By then Kendra would be home from class and would get him ready for bed. They'd all reunite for the nightly bath-time battle, in which Gene would delightedly pit himself against the grownups for a water massacre to rival that of Salamis, and then Kendra would tuck him into bed, as Adam and Maren went off by themselves.

Despite his initial reservations, Adam had found that he enjoyed their habitual closeness, skin against skin, ready for sleep. Perhaps this marriage could be beneficial in more ways than one. He cared deeply for Maren and could think of no one else with whom he'd attempt such a foolhardy endeavor, but for a man with such specific neurological requirements, perhaps it was a good step for him as well. Expanding his world. Adjusting his routine. Bending his rules.

It was much harder to get lost in his own head when there was a person sleeping beside him. Then again…it was much harder to escape into his own head when there was a person sleeping beside him.

It was a give and take.

Adam marched up the walkway with a sigh. He was sure there would be no sleeping tonight, only fighting. Pointed accusations and vague deflections. He'd already missed nine calls from her.

"I'm home," he called as he pushed open the door, gearing up for battle. "Maren, before you start, there are still things we didn't know about each other from before, things I was working on, and you can't take umbrage with them now just because—"

She appeared from the kitchen, clutching a phone with red-rimmed eyes.

Adam froze. Oh God. This was going to be worse than he thought.

"Maren, please, I—"

"It's not that, Adam, even though we'll talk about that later. I've been trying to call you." She hugged the phone tighter and looked at him with uncertainty. "It's your father."

The next morning, Adam was on a flight to Montana.

It was cancer, he had been told. An invasive malignancy that had progressed quickly to the end stages, landing his father in the ICU. Adam flipped through SkyMall and picked weakly at his breakfast. He hadn't even known his father was sick.

His parents had divorced around the same time Adam left for college and his life picked up a sudden speed. He'd moved from the safety net of his family to the much preferred safety net of the lab. Now he seldom heard from either parent, and only had a cool, distant relationship with his father, who had remarried and remained on the family ranch.

As they began their initial descent into Glacier Park, Adam was seized with a sudden panic. Not about seeing his father in the hospital, but about the three little vials stowed safely in his bag.

The idea had come to him last night as he'd been packing. The timing was perfect, and no one would ever know. It may be considered unethical, but surely his father wouldn't mind. And more importantly, Adam would never get a chance like this again.

So in addition to his change of clothes and toiletries, he'd carefully packed three syringes of his immune factor, prepared by cloning the B lymphocytes in Gene's blood.

When the plane touched down, Adam rented a car from the airport and drove to the hospital in Kalispell. He got an update from the doctor, and the nurses pointed him to the right room. There were no other visitors, and his stepmother had apparently gone home to shower and get a few hours of rest. That was a shame; Adam had been hoping for a sort of conversational buffer.

Instead, he took a deep breath, smoothed his jacket, and for the first time in over five years, Adam prepared to see his father.

But all he could see were the tubes.

He stopped short, unprepared for the flood of pain and fear that washed over him. His father was there somewhere, buried under all the machinery, and he was going to die.

"Would you stop stalling? I'm not gone yet."

Adam jumped in his skin and stared back into the sharp eyes looking up at him from a dent in the hospital pillow. He tried to smile, but it was just a grimace as he pulled up a chair and took a seat beside the bed.

"How are you feeling, Dad?"

The old man laughed, coughing as he did. "Great! Never better! Glad to see all that schooling paid off, Adam; you're still sharp as a tack."

Adam grinned. "So are you."

And he truly was. Despite the severity of his diagnosis, his father was still amazingly alert and stable, almost as if a huge tumor wasn't destroying his pancreas.

"So how have you been, Adam?"

Adam looked at his hands, feeling guilty of his sudden success. "I'm fine. I published a scientific paper two days ago…it's making a bit of a splash."

His father regarded him patiently. "Yes, yes I heard about that. But what's the *other* news?"

Adam went blank. "The *other* news?"

"I have a grandson!"

"Oh." Adam recovered quickly. "Yes, that."

"Yes. *That.*" Hopeful crinkles creased around the old man's eyes. "Do you have any pictures?"

Pictures of his son. That would make sense.

Adam really wished he had made a checklist of all these normal parental things to do so he wouldn't keep getting caught unawares.

He made a show of reaching for his wallet. "Uh, I think I left it in my hurry to get over here. But he's a good kid. I named him Gene."

"Gene. Good family name," the old man reproached sarcastically.

Adam rolled his eyes. "We can't all be 'Walter,' and I wouldn't do that to a child."

Not unless it had some kind of scientific significance.

His father laughed again and promptly dissolved in a fit of wheezes and coughs.

Adam frowned and handed him a small cup of water. "I'm going to go talk to your doctors and see if we can get you moved home. How does that sound?"

Walter closed his eyes. "That would be heaven. I want to see the ranch again. That's where I want to be when it happens."

Adam's throat closed and he nodded stiffly before getting to his feet and sweeping from the room. Once he was

68

safely out of sight, he leaned back against the wall and covered his eyes with his hands. Hopefully his father wouldn't have to suffer through this much longer. Adam's mind travelled to his hotel room, where the three little vials were packed safely away.

Hopefully, he had found a solution.

"Dr. Barfield, are you all right? Can I get you anything?"

A kindly nurse rested a hand on his shoulder and he quickly pulled himself together.

"Yes. I'd like to speak to someone about hospice care. My father would like to spend the rest of his remaining time at home."

Two nights later a hospital bed was moved into his father's bedroom at the ranch. A team of nurses was scheduled to come at regular intervals to feed, medicate, turn, and bathe him. They kept a detailed list of a dozen different pills and injections duct taped to the refrigerator. No one was to touch the list, and it was to be adhered to with something close to reverence. When Walter died, it would be from his cancer, not medical malfeasance.

Of course, there was one medication that was not on the list. One that only Adam knew about.

He'd given Walter the first injection when he was still in the hospital. After he'd arranged for hospice care, he'd crept back into the room while his father slept and injected the lymphocytes directly into his IV.

The next injection had been the first morning back at the ranch. This time, he'd simply presented it like one of the multiple other medications his father was prescribed, and had administered it as they discussed the local high school's football season.

There had been no visible changes in his father's condition. In fact, if anything, his pain had continued to worsen, and he now required an oxygen tank to help him breathe.

Adam watched these events transpire with almost palpable agitation. If only he could get his father back to the lab for study. Whatever changes Gene's blood was facilitating were surely happening on a micro-cellular level within the cancer cells themselves. Adam had already stayed longer than he had planned, and would soon have to return to the university and his lab.

What if he was unable to see the plan to the finish? What if there was an improvement, a dying back of the malignant tumor that Adam was unable to advertise? Or even worse, what if his father died?

Adam would mourn a while, as would any dutiful son, but the larger implications of Walter's passing would be far more severe. It would prove the B lymphocytes in Gene's blood were ineffective. All the study and medical research Adam had been sweating over for the last few months would be in vain. The scientific community would not get its promised breakthrough.

And Adam would never earn his place among the greats.

These thoughts plagued him, until at last, he administered the final injection and decided he had to go. It would happen, or it wouldn't. His father would live, or he would die. There was nothing he could do about it now.

With what could be final farewells, Adam headed back for Glacier Park and caught a return flight to SFO.

Maren, Kendra, Lilly, and Gene had done well during his absence. In fact, the house had continued running so smoothly, it begged the question, what exactly did Adam contribute to the family dynamic?

Maren got up to greet him with a tight embrace the second he walked in the door.

"How's he doing?" she asked softly.

Adam eased away and kissed her quickly on the forehead. "We'll wait and see."

Lilly jumped to her feet and hurried over as well. "Adam, I'm so sorry. When Maren told us about your dad, I—"

Maren cut her off sharply. "Lilly, watch the baby. Adam and I are going to unpack."

Adam glanced between them, bewildered by the sudden tension, as Maren took him firmly by the hand and led him to their bedroom. After two exhaustive hours of answering questions about his father and watching Maren dance around asking about his research paper, Adam was finally allowed to turn off the lights and say goodnight.

Every muscle and over-excited nerve ending in his body ached for rest. It seemed as though he had been running without stopping for the last year, ever since he got that ultrasound picture in the mail. His tidy, quiet life had transformed into a spectacle, and even the safety of his own bed had been overrun.

He turned on his side, facing away from Maren, and wondered how everything had gotten away from him so quickly. And quite possibly, for nothing. If the B lymphocytes in Gene's blood had no effect, then all of this had been a waste of time.

Using a silent breathing technique he hadn't done since childhood to help him calm down, Adam was finally able to close his eyes and fall into a fitful sleep. But what seemed like a second later, he was awakened once more by the phone.

He groped around blindly in the dark until he finally came up with the receiver. "What?" he answered irritably. Then his whole faced changed and he bolted up and turned on the light.

"Dad?"

Chapter 8

Adam stared at the page of results in front of him. The director of care at Kalispell Memorial had faxed it over. One page, and yet it encapsulated a lifetime's worth of achievement.

Gene's blood had worked. Adam's immunity serum was a success.

He had gotten the call late last night, and to say that the hospice director was a little worked up would be underselling it. He had never seen results like this before, and medically speaking, he didn't know how to explain it. It was a miracle!

Well Adam certainly knew how to explain it.

He was able to use his excitement over his father's astonishing recovery to thwart Maren for a few more days regarding the discussion of his paper, but he knew the time was coming. In the meanwhile, he spent every waking second he had at the lab.

Additional calls and faxes from his father's physicians had revealed that not only had the cancer stopped its progression, but it had actually regressed to the point where it was no longer evident with any test or scan. His father had "flunked out" of hospice.

Adam was almost light-headed with euphoria. Everything he'd theorized had come true. Not only the AIDS virus, but now several groupings of cancer cells had yielded to the cloned B lymphocytes. Gene's blood was like magic.

But every bright moment was paired with the dark acknowledgment. None of this mattered, because he couldn't tell anyone.

He couldn't publish, nor did his research mean anything in a clinical trial. In order for it not to slip forgotten between the pages of history, it required some credence or authenticity. If he could join a group already functioning and finding results, it would give him a leg up on legitimacy, but no group would have him without a basis from which to establish his work.

They wanted to know the donor. And that was something that Adam couldn't give them.

With a heavy heart, he dragged himself home from the train station. His work at the lab today had been astounding. His data was off the charts. He'd summarized everything in yet another groundbreaking article…and he had half a mind to throw it away.

What was the point? Why strive for greatness when you'd have to enjoy it from behind bars?

But it was not in Adam to stop. If there were still questions on the table, then he would keep working. Until all the tests were complete and all the results were analyzed, he'd be in the lab.

And to do that, he would need more blood.

He pushed open the door and was hit with the smell of pizza. Pizza and wine. Maren had prepared their favorite dinner. Clearly, she wanted to talk.

Lilly was off for the night, and Kendra was still at school, so that would just leave the three of them. Adam heard pots and pans bustling about in the kitchen as Maren unloaded the dishwasher, and he decided now was as good a time as any to get his sample from Gene.

The child was playing alone in the living room in a circle of his own toys. He didn't look up when Adam came towards him; he was used to being ignored by the man. But the second that Adam pulled a syringe out of his pocket, the strangest thing happened.

Adam twisted off the cap and looked up to see Gene staring directly at him, holding a building block frozen in the air. Then, with a movement so deliberate it sent chills careening up Adam's spine, Gene tucked his foot squarely underneath his little leg.

Adam stopped where he was as the two held direct eye contact.

How could he know? He was too young to make the connection. And the Pavlovian way in which he cringed away from Adam was forever seared into his brain.

"What are you two doing?"

Adam whirled around to see Maren standing in the corner with her arms folded across her chest. Gene returned to his toys and the professor quickly slipped the empty syringe into his pocket.

"When did he get that shirt?" he asked, gesturing to the Lion King monstrosity plastered across his son's chest.

Maren rolled her eyes. "Kendra got it for him. I think she's in love."

Adam chuckled nervously. "What's not to love?"

"Come on." Maren gestured to the kitchen. "I ordered dinner."

***

Adam sank stiffly into a chair at the table, and Maren followed every movement with her eyes. It had been like this ever since the article was published—*he* had been like this. He hung his head and walked as though the weight of the world was on his shoulders. And Maren truly didn't understand why. He'd made a scientific breakthrough, the kind of revelation that would be studied by others as fundamental groundwork in a brand new field. It was the dream.

So why was he so unhappy?

She wanted to help, to carry some of the load, but Adam had never been one to let people in. It would be up to her, the adult with some empathetic capacity, to reassure him. It would fall on her to hold this family together, and help him fight whatever demons were chasing him. After all, that was what marriage was all about, right? Supporting each other through everything?

She sat down at the opposite end of the table and was about to reach for the wine when Adam suddenly stood.

"Look Maren, I know this is going to be a big thing, but I have to tell you—"

"I don't care," she interrupted. He fell silent, looking stunned, and she was quick to repeat herself. "I don't care that you didn't tell me about the paper. Your work is your own Adam, it's always been that way. I don't expect any different."

***

Perhaps it was that this unexpected forgiveness had caught him off guard. Perhaps it was that he simply couldn't hold it in any longer. But a part of Adam's veneer suddenly cracked.

"I can't tell people who the donor is."

The words rang out in between them and echoed into silence.

"Yes," Maren frowned, "you said that in your interviews. You won't—"

"No—*can't*." Adam's breathing was very shallow as he tried to make her understand. "I can't tell them, Maren."

She stared at him blankly for a moment, trying to understand, before it suddenly clicked.

Her eyebrows shot up, and she looked down at her empty plate. "Oh."

Adam's heart pounded in his throat as his eyes raked over every inch of her face, trying to gauge her reaction. She wasn't giving him much to go on, and he felt as though he might explode.

"And I can't tell you either. I mean—I shouldn't. So I won't."

She glanced up and spoke mildly. "No, I guess it's probably best that you don't."

They lapsed back into silence and Adam wondered if he actually might be having a mild heart attack. But then, all at once, Maren smiled. Their eyes met and Adam held his breath.

"You told me," she said, her eyes glowing warmly. "You...you let me know."

***

You let me in.

That was what she really wanted to say. But she didn't want to scare him off. It was enough for her. This much was enough.

She was infatuated. Completely taken with the man sitting before her. They had been a team once, back in the lab, and she would make sure that they were a team again. So she couldn't know the exact derivation of the blood? Fine. It didn't matter where it had come from, blood was blood. She could work with him all the same.

"Let's eat," she said, ripping open the box of pizza. "The food's getting cold."

***

Several times throughout the course of dinner, Adam found himself staring inexplicably across the table at Maren's thoughtful face. She had said no more about the paper, and did nothing to press him, but he could tell, just by looking at her, that she would still be willing to help. He had found a true ally the day he hired Maren as his TA. And in doing so, he had made a true friend.

The more he stared, the more he was convinced. This wedding was going to be one of the best things that had ever happened to him.

If you had asked Adam that same question a few months later, his answer might have changed.

"And remember, you need to pick up the new vest for Gene's tuxedo from the tailors."

Adam closed his eyes and silently smashed his head repeatedly against his desk.

After their talk, his relationship with Maren had soared to new heights. She had backed away from asking probing questions, but spent countless hours in the lab helping with the grunt work and discussing the finer points of his study. And while Adam found it useful to have another brain to bounce things off, the price was proving painfully high.

"Why does he need *another* vest?" he mumbled into his papers.

She swept past the office door. "Because he grew out of his old one." There was a rattling in the kitchen and her voice grew louder. "In fact, Adam, can you take him with you? I'm going to need the space to get ready with the girls."

78

Adam threw down his pencil in a silent rage. Of course she needed the space. In fact, Adam would like some space too. And some *quiet*.

He rubbed his eyes. "Of course I can. We'll just meet you there."

She poked her head inside and Adam was officially seeing red. "Are you sure? You didn't want to go over the vows again?"

He struggled to control his temper. "We're repeating what the minister says, Maren. We're echoing it back to him. Honestly, a monkey could do it."

Monkeys!

He looked at his clock in utter dismay while simultaneously jamming his arms in the wrong holes in his jacket and trying to pick up his briefcase.

His lab was getting a shipment of a dozen macaques today, curtesy of the World Health Organization, who was eager to help him advance his trials in whatever limited way possible. Like everyone else, they were puzzled by his seemingly self-imposed roadblock, but they had seen glimpses of the science, and the work he was doing was too important to quit.

"I've got to get to the lab," he gasped, grabbing his things, "I need to be there when the test subjects arrive!"

Maren folded her arms across her chest. "Honestly Adam, of all the days."

Indeed, Maren—*of all the days*. He whirled around, but wisely held his tongue, forcing himself instead to smile.

"I'll be there, on time, with Gene. My tux is already in the car." He kissed her forehead and she slowly relaxed into a smile. "Everything's going to be fine. You have nothing to worry about."

"Nothing's going to be fine!" Adam panted, as he raced up the familiar streets to the university, Gene strapped obliviously in his car seat. "I just got a text from Terry that we have twelve primates as ordered, but only ten cages were delivered. Your new favorite game is to guilt me about taking a little blood. The W.H.O. is breathing down my neck for the first batch of results, and I have to tell them they need to wait a few weeks while I go on a blasted honeymoon!"

They screeched to a stop in Adam's assigned parking space.

"Of all the days for Maren to want to get married."

He glanced in the rear view mirror to see Gene blinking innocently back at him.

"I'll give you this, kid, you're a good listener."

Inside the lab, things were no less chaotic. Ten monkeys screamed and rattled the bars of their cages, while two more ran around on leashes, dragging their frantic handlers behind them. Terry, the man in charge of the primates, looked like he was on the verge of tears by the time Adam came racing up to him, little Gene in tow.

"What are you doing?" Adam demanded, setting Gene down to stand beside him. "The holding room is on the other side of Leffler Hall. They're not supposed to be awake in the lab."

Katie, one of Adam's grad students, slapped a monkey's hand as it reached covertly for her granola. "Professor?"

"Yes, Katie, I'm taking care of it."

Tim, another upper level, pulled open the door and seemed to barely notice the spectacle as he made his way routinely to his table. "Finally, the freshman interns are here."

"Dr. Barfield, where should we put the ones without cages?"

The larger of the two hopped up on Katie's desk, still trying to get the granola. When she snatched it away, it ripped through her notes in protest. "Professor!"

"Yes Katie! I'm taking care of it!"

Tim located the smaller monkey and began a friendly game of catch.

"Dr. Barfield?"

Adam's phone buzzed in his pocket, and he held up a finger. "Hang on a second." He flipped open the phone. "Yes dear?" His face clouded and he held the receiver a little farther away from his ear. "Yes—I got Gene's tux. Yes—we're on our way to the church." There was a pause while he listened and his face flushed defensively. "I'm sorry, Maren, but we had a problem with some of the monkeys!"

"Monkeys," Gene giggled.

The sound in the room seemed to stop. All the adults turned to look at the child, and even the smaller monkey wandered over and appraised him thoughtfully. Gene giggled again at the animal, squeezing Adam's fingers as he started mimicking its sound and motions. He looked up to Adam for approval, and Adam stared back, at a loss, his eyes roving between the test monkey and his little son, mirroring each other's every move.

All at once his heart seized up. "Stop doing that!" he snapped fiercely. Gene looked up in despair and started to cry.

The spell was broken, and the room became a wall of sound once more.

"Dr. Barfield, I really need to know where to put these monkeys!"

"Was that Gene's first word? Isn't he way too young to be talking?"

"Professor, it got my granola!"

81

"Adam." Adam whirled around to see Keven McDonale wading towards him through the fray, frowning at his watch. "Don't you need to get going?"

Ten minutes and two monkey attacks later, Adam and Gene were heading for the church. Adam kept glancing back in the mirror at the little boy. He couldn't get the image out of his head; his experimental monkey and Gene, acting as perfect reflections. He shook his head to clear it as they pulled up to the sanctuary and grabbed Gene out of the back, straightening their tuxes before racing inside.

Maren had planned a fairy tale wedding. Little Gene was carried up to the altar by both Kendra and Lilly, who glided down the aisle with matching dresses of green velvet. Hundreds of red and white flowers cascaded down from the high ceilings under which Adam stood, somewhat begrudgingly, in a dark tuxedo with a green cummerbund and a boutonniere of ironically appropriate narcissus. Kendra looked back at Adam—she was haunted by the Greek myth telling of Narcissus living to a wise old age if he never discovered self-knowledge.

The music started and everyone stood as Maren floated slowly towards him, positively glowing in a breathtaking designer town. The white satin hugged her closely around the bodice before flowing out from a high empire waste. Her veil was imported Italian lace, fitted into her hair by an eighty-year-old mother of pearl pin belonging to her grandmother.

Sure enough, Adam and Maren chanted back their vows with hardly a thought; their eyes were only on each other. The minister pronounced them, and with a fleeting kiss, they bound their lives together forever.

The small gathering cheered before heading to the reception for food and dance. None of Adam's family was present — they were too busy thanking the Lord for Walter's miraculous recovery — but Maren had brought a large group of people from the city, and several of her and Adam's colleagues were in attendance as well.

Little Gene was passed from person to person, charming everyone with his miniature white tuxedo and sparkling blue eyes. Adam watched him, almost warily, until Maren took him gently by the arm.

"This is the happiest day of my life, Adam."

Adam closed his eyes and leaned his cheek against her head. He had to admit, though he had balked at some of the ritual and expense, it had been a beautiful ceremony.

"Mine too." He felt Maren smile.

"Not only did I marry the man I love," her eyes fell on Gene, "but I'm getting a family as well."

Adam followed her gaze. "He said his first word today, you know."

She pulled away in amazement. "So soon? What was it?"

Adam thought back to the startling moment and felt the sudden impulse to lie. "Mama."

Her eyes teared up and she rushed to scoop him out of the arms of his adoring fans. Adam was watching the two of them when there was a sudden clap on his shoulder. He looked up and had to smile. McDonale had three small scratches on the side of his cheek, and a bruise was already forming below his left eye. He clutched hard at his whiskey while his hand spastically tremored.

"I have to hand it to you; I never gave you science guys enough credit." He downed the whiskey in a single gulp. "It's a jungle out there."

Adam laughed. "What did you end up doing with the loose monkeys?"

"We put them in your students' locker room. We didn't think they'd mind."

They chuckled to themselves as they watched the women fawning over Gene.

"Whole new chapter of your life starting." McDonale grinned mischievously as Maren eyed the baby with obvious longing. "You ready for it?"

Adam grabbed his own whiskey off a passing tray and threw it back.

"I guess we're about to find out."

Chapter 9

After a brief trip down to Monterey, where Adam and Maren enjoyed themselves as newlyweds, they arrived back in Berkeley to find the weather dark and foreboding. A light rain dampened their hair and chilled them as they grabbed their bags out of the cab and hurried inside.

"Look who's home!" Lilly gushed as she nudged Gene forward. He took a few wobbling steps before Maren snatched him up in her arms.

"Well hello there, little man! And how was your week?" she cooed, kissing his forehead.

"Everything went great," Lilly answered. "You got a message from a guy named Terry; said some of the monkeys staged a coup at the lab, but that everything's under control."

Adam set down his bags with a groan and leaned heavily against the wall. "Of course they did."

Lilly wrinkled her nose. "I don't get it...why do you have to experiment on animals?"

Maren smoothed down Gene's wavy hair. "Because animals are like us."

"...then why is it morally okay to experiment on animals?"

This time, it was Adam who replied. "Because animals are not like us. Such is the inherent flaw in scientific explanation."

He smiled courteously at Lilly, with a cautious glance at Maren, before grabbing a mug of coffee and heading to his study. Maren set Gene down and stared after him with confusion.

"Adam, aren't we going to get some dinner? Spend time with Gene?"

Finally reunited with his work, Adam set down the mug on his desk and opened up his laptop to begin checking emails. "You guys order whatever you like. I'm going to get to it."

There was a hushed conversation and a few seconds later, Maren quietly pushed open the door and slipped inside. Glancing quickly to make sure there was nothing on his desk she shouldn't see, Adam half-closed his laptop and peered up at her over the edge.

"What is it? Is something wrong?"

She perched tentatively on the edge of his desk. "It's just...we only just got home, Adam. You haven't seen your son in over a week, and the first thing you do is dive straight into work?"

Adam's thin layer of patience finally broke.

"Have you not been paying attention? I've done what you asked. I made you my wife! We're married now, and you have the perfect home, with the perfect family. What more do you want?"

Maren's face paled. "I want to help. We're a team, Adam. I thought we'd come to an understanding...."

"Well, you can't," he said shortly. "You're only an assistant professor, Maren. You're just starting out; you have no experience. This is my project and therefore, it's my problem."

He re-opened his laptop, callously ignoring her devastated face. In the living room, Gene heard their raised voices and started crying. The sound grated on Adam, and he winced before downing his coffee and glaring back at the monitor.

"Actually I take that back." He began typing an email. "There is something you can do."

Maren slowly raised her head, looking numbed and hurt.

"Tend to the baby."

The next morning, Adam woke up to a letter on his pillow. He'd snuck into bed at around four a.m., exhausted, yet painfully aware of how much damage he'd caused. There was no sign of Maren anywhere, and Adam reached for the envelope with a sinking feeling in his gut.

But what he read didn't make sense.

The door opened and he looked up with a start to see Maren holding two coffees. As she settled herself on the bed, he held out the letter in bewilderment.

"What's this?"

Maren sipped her own coffee and set Adam's down on the nightstand. "Well, I knew that we needed to test in a human population, and since you said that we're operating outside the guidelines of the United States and most European countries, I contacted the department of health in Kahlu."

Adam shook his head, trying to understand. "Africa?"

Maren's eyes narrowed slightly. "That's right. They have a village on the northwestern border that's in a full blown

AIDS epidemic. About eighty-percent of adult males are already infected, and the numbers are getting worse every day. I faxed over a copy of your article as well as some of our more recent data, and the government promised to fund a small clinic, authorized us to get a control group, and gave us a six-month window to carry out a trial with your vaccine."

Adam's jaw dropped. "I can't believe...how did you even...?"

Maren let him flounder for a moment, sipping her espresso. "I used to be quite the scientist myself, *professor*."

Adam blinked. His eyes travelled slowly between the letter and Maren's face, before settling on his caffeine. He took a couple of desperate gulps, trying to clear his head, but came up blank.

"You're an amazing woman."

Maren was taken aback, but smiled, looking pleased.

"I'm not going to apologize for worrying about you," she said softly. "I'm not going to apologize for trying to do what's best for this family."

"I know." Adam set down their drinks and pulled her closer. "I'm sorry. I'm just so stressed with the animal tests and how we're ever going to take it to the next level."

Maren slapped him gently on the face with the letter. "Well, problem solved."

He kissed her passionately. "It most certainly is."

They pulled an inch or so apart, breathing heavily, before Adam threw a pillow to close the door.

Then he kissed her some more.

It only took about three weeks to nail down the logistics before the big trip. Adam had to secure a temporary replacement for his classes, and Maren worked to make sure conditions were set up for housing and the clinic. The old housekeeper was fired, and Maren took the new one through the ropes before leaving her a spare set of keys.

The worst part of it all were the multiple vaccines Adam, Gene, Maren, and Kendra all had to take before the flight. Never before had any of them heard such a horrific scream as when little Gene saw the doctor approaching with the needle.

The next morning, the little troupe scarfed down a quick breakfast and began loading their things into the car. Maren and Adam worried about the details while Kendra was assigned to keep the baby calm.

"Are you ready to go to Africa?" she asked him playfully.

Gene grinned from ear to ear. "Monkeys!"

Kendra's face crinkled with confusion. "Um...yeah. Monkeys."

They were just about ready to go when Lilly sped around the corner and parked her aged Camry against the curb. She had decided to stay in Berkeley to finish out the semester, but it hadn't been an easy decision. The second the car was stopped she jumped out, threw a quick goodbye to Kendra, and jogged up the walkway to where Adam was holding Gene.

"I just couldn't let you leave without saying goodbye!" She leaned down and kissed Gene softly on the forehead. "I'm going to miss this little guy so much." A few tears slid silently down her face. "I just...don't want to be forgotten." She looked up with feeling. "Do you understand what I'm saying, Adam?"

Their eyes met and he brushed her hair gently off her shoulder. "No one is forgetting you."

Maren started honking incessantly from the car and they pulled apart.

Nine hours and eight Tylenol later, they were halfway across the world. Their adventure had officially begun.

The arrangements made for them in Kuhlu left little to be desired. They had a small, tidy house with beds enclosed in fresh mosquito netting, as well as a nice, compact little office from which to analyze their research and results. In addition, the director of the health program had hired a sweet young woman to cook, translate, and clean.

While Kendra stayed behind to settle in with Gene, Adam and Maren walked the forty yards to their new clinic. The lack of adequately supplied medical facilities had historically made treating AIDS in Africa extremely difficult. But this was a fully equipped, mobile HIV/AIDS health clinic. The inside was clean and the instruments were sterile. Set up alongside was a similar treatment center that would help educate the victims and their families about the transmission of HIV/AIDS, as well as providing some needed health care. A small team of medical professionals, most of whom could speak at least broken English, were there to help the Barfields with whatever the study required. All in all, it was a perfect setup.

Their first task was to recruit testing applicants. They needed twenty-one healthy subjects, and another matched group who were in the advanced stage of illness. It was vital to recruit people who were not taking other medications, and surprisingly enough, even more than the language barrier, this proved to be the most difficult obstacle so far. Adam and Maren spent most nights debating as to whether the locally administered herbs and potions would be classified as medications. They had to turn away countless applicants, but in the end, both groups met their requirements and they were finally able to begin the actual trial.

It was an exciting time for Adam and Maren, but the work itself was exhausting. They would come home every night with scarcely enough energy to bathe before bed. On the other hand, Gene would be positively bursting with excitement and Kendra would be dying for an adult to talk to.

The first week they were there, she'd taken the baby on what the health director had promised would be a casual trip to the city to see the sights and show Gene the countryside. What actually transpired was a tragic series of events which left them wandering around for hours, scared and lost, until a kindly farmer had returned them to the clinic.

After that, they tended to stay inside.

"Well, if it weren't for the bugs, the snakes, the spiders, and the fact that everyone in this country is dying of AIDS, I could really see us settling down here." Maren patted her damp hair with a towel and settled cross-legged onto the bed.

Within seconds, Gene was on her lap, demanding to be entertained. He'd developed an unfortunate habit of trying to climb the mosquito netting, which was held in place now only with a delicate system of duct tape. He eyed it mischievously and Maren was quick to divert him.

"What do you think, Adam? Shall we set up shop?"

Adam emerged from the shower as well, scratching furiously at a series of spider bites he'd somehow contracted while walking between the house and the clinic.

"Oh yes," he said sarcastically. "We'll at least get a time share." He plopped down on the bed beside them and stretched out his limbs. "I'd forgotten how much the 'hands on' work takes it out of you. On your feet ten hours a day...."

Maren giggled. "I'm sorry, Professor. Missing the office? Wishing you could delegate to the low-life labor force like me? If only Tim could see you now."

He chuckled and ducked as she hit him with a pillow. "At least the trial is going well."

It certainly was. They were conducting a double blind trial where half the subjects got the real medicine, and the other half got the placebo. Each and every result was painstakingly recorded, but between the Barfields and the rest of the research team, they were right on schedule.

During the first week, both groups were given injections on alternate days. During the second week, nothing was given. The third week was more alternating injections, and during the fourth week, they waited and observed.

The last week was like torture. The opportunity for a trial like this came along once in a lifetime, and if the results failed to warrant further study, they would be shut down forever.

Maren actually prepared a special breakfast in honor of the occasion — the day they were supposed to receive the first batch of data. The small family gathered around their slanted table, and offered a silent prayer to the gods of science. Please let this be a success!

The dream was to be undetectable. That simply meant that there was no longer enough virus in the subjects for the tests to locate and count. But Adam and Maren would settle for a lot less than undetectable. Even if their medicine was able to halt the progression of the disease, it would still be considered a grand triumph.

The Kuhla health department had sent over a representative to oversee the results of the trial, and they all stood together and held their breath as the antiquated printer spat out the first page of numbers into Adam's trembling hand.

His eyes glassed over as he stared at the columns of data. This couldn't be right.

"Well." Maren was standing on her toes, hands clasped together. "What does it say?!"

He stared up at her in a daze. "…undetectable."

She frowned and grabbed the paper out of his hand. "No it doesn't." There was a split second's silence as her mouth fell open and tears fell down her cheeks. "Yes it does. Oh my God, Adam."

"*Undetectable!*" he yelled, shaking everyone in the tiny space.

Maren screamed and jumped onto him, wrapping her legs around him as she kissed him all over the face. The health representative plucked the paper out of her fingers and looked it over for himself, utterly astonished by the results in his hand.

"I can't believe it!" he exclaimed. "You did it, Dr. Barfield! Not a trace of the virus anywhere!"

With that the little clinic emptied. People got on the phone and on the computer, rushing to tell everyone they could about the miraculous trial. Within minutes, the NIH was demanding complete documentation, and immediately sent over a request that Adam write another research paper to be delivered to the Biotechnology Industry Organization the following month. Adam's father was informed by a random clinic worker with an accent so thick, Adam felt sure Walter didn't get the message. Even the dean received and quickly returned an email congratulating Adam on his unbelievable success.

But amidst the flurry of activity, Adam and Maren stayed perfectly still, embracing in the center of the busy room.

"You did it, honey," she murmured into his hair. "I'm so proud of you."

Adam stared again at the page of results over her head, unable to comprehend how his life had changed so dramatically.

Everything would be different now. The money. The prestige. The next trial. Things were just getting started. And they would have options. Every medical organization in the world was going to want to be a part of this. "Barfield's magical serum," as it was already being called unofficially, was the most significant step forward in genetics and medicine in the last hundred years.

The only remaining question was the donor. Where had he gotten the lymphocytes? What was the source?

Adam thought of little Gene, just forty paces away, playing with the mosquito netting and completely oblivious to the world around him.

If only they knew....

Chapter 10

The press was calling all their stops. The news was stupendous, and the scientific world was at Adam's doorstep. He maintained a cool, aloof attitude, and explained with great patience the precise method of cloning the B interferon. But he refused to share the identity of the donor. He was almost starting to feel like a reporter himself, giving everything he had to protect his source.

But at least for now, it seemed to be sufficient.

After making such progress against the devastation wreaked by AIDS, Adam turned his attention towards human testing in those with advanced cancer. There were many clinics in Mexico that were offering unproven approaches, and Adam contacted several of these as a preliminary step towards setting up a similar trial to what he and Maren had conducted in Africa. He received a dozen positive responses, and soon flew down in person to deliver the vaccine along with instructions for its use. Now all he had to do was sit back and wait for the results.

Meanwhile, his ongoing anthropological study on Gene was progressing at rapid rates. The boy was a dynamo; no sooner had he settled on one plane of development than he was already shooting off to the next. He was beginning to walk and talk with increasing confidence, sometimes making up words of his own when the English language seemed to fail him. He'd been successfully weaned from Kendra and only saw her now on a limited basis. These days, Lilly was in charge. She was a patient teacher, playing tapes in French and Spanish, introducing him to classical music, and honing motor skills and basis manners. She'd even gotten him mostly toilet trained.

Absolutely no physical evidence of his unique genetic background was apparent, and despite being a virtual lab rat, he was a happy, loving boy. A toddler who would soon be starting preschool; a huge step forward, as Gene seldom got to play and interact with anyone his own age.

Adam recorded everything in a detailed journal, clocking things like his height, weight, reflexes, preferences, stamina, and response time.

Tests like these were easy enough to perform while still avoiding notice. He'd call Gene inside to play, only to be measuring the time it took him to respond with a stopwatch. He'd shine flashlights in his eyes to test his reactions, and prick his fingers to gauge his reflexes. He'd even held his hand under icy water to see how long it would take him to cry.

***

But while it was easy enough to deceive Gene, a trusting two-year-old, Maren was another story.

It was hard to ignore that whenever Gene came inside from playing with Daddy, he would always seem to have a little bruise, or twitch, or most times, be on the verge of tears. Maren wasn't sure if it was just that boys tended to play rougher, or if Adam's challenges with Asperger's were making it difficult for him to pay attention to the emotional state of the child. But most days, she was just happy that Adam was paying attention to Gene at all.

Poor little Gene was being reared by women, and while that left him sweet and loving, he needed a father. But Adam showed very little interest in parenting beyond an observational role. It was almost as if he didn't even consider himself to be Gene's father. He never interacted with him in a close and personal way, and the more Gene seemed to blossom, the more Adam pulled back.

Maren had tried every trick she knew to try to rouse Adam's interest. She'd planned family outings, left him alone to babysit, and even insisted that they go on weekly drives together, but nothing seemed to work. It was as though Adam just didn't love him. Maybe he couldn't.

Maren was lost in these very thoughts one Sunday morning when Lilly came bustling into the house. Gene ran over to meet her and she scooped him up and kissed him before waving hello to Maren and heading to the kitchen to pack up supplies.

Every weekend she took Gene to the San Francisco Zoo. It was an all day trip that was unquestionably Gene's favorite thing in the world. He would ride his stroller onto BART before toddling alongside it at the zoo as he and Lilly looked at the different animals and talked about what sounds they made. Next would come a ride on the Little Puffer, the zoo's miniature train, before the visit would end with a few rounds on the big carousel by the duck pond.

Usually, if he was good, Gene could weasel himself some ice cream between activities.

He clapped his little hands and stomped his little feet in excitement, clambering around and getting in Lilly's way as she pilfered through the cupboards for juice and crackers.

"Calm down, little man, or we'll never get there!"

Maren leaned in the doorway and watched them prepare, still thinking about Adam. And speak of the devil, at that very moment, there was a crash followed by a loud yelping from somewhere deep in the house. The next second, Adam appeared in the kitchen, wringing coffee out of his shirt and looking decidedly bashful.

"There was a spill…," he began, searching for the paper towels to clean it.

Maren had a sudden thought. "Let me!" She grabbed the towels off the microwave and picked up a bottle of soap. "And why don't you go to the zoo with Gene and Lilly?"

The activity in the kitchen paused as Adam looked at Maren in confusion. "I was waiting for the results from the Mexican trial; I should really stick around—"

"Exactly," she cut him off, "you're *waiting*. You can do that anywhere. Go. Spend time with your son. It'll be good for you."

He started to protest, but she silenced him with a long look.

"Go."

***

A day at the zoo wasn't as bad as Adam thought it would be. He took his journal with him and trailed along behind the other two as they visited the animals and rode the little train. Gene was delighted with the additional company, holding tightly onto both of his protectors' hands, and Adam had to admit, he was enjoying spending time with Lilly as well.

When he'd returned from Africa, he was thrilled to find that things picked up right where they'd left off. There were no hassles with Lilly, no expectations. The sex was great, and as long as Maren never found out, Adam didn't see the harm in indulging himself every now and again.

Together, they lifted Gene between them for a mighty swing and he erupted in a fit of laughter.

The sun was high in the sky as they climbed the grassy bank by the duck pond. Families had spread out blankets for picnics and euphoric dogs ran back and forth chasing Frisbees. It was a Norman Rockwell. But Adam was surprised to find that he didn't mind it in the least. Quite the contrary. For the first time in a long series of months, Adam was actually having fun.

The second they reached the top of the little hill, Lilly suddenly dropped to her knees in front of Gene. The child's face lit up with wild glee, but he kept his mouth shut, eyes twinkling as if he knew what was coming next.

"I think I'm forgetting something...." Lilly gave an exaggerated frown. "Gene, do you know what it is?"

Gene practically jumped off the ground in excitement. "*Ice cream!*"

Lilly continued to puzzle. "I just can't seem to remember. Could you help me out?"

"ICE CREAM!"

"Oh, yeah." She grinned and got to her feet. "Ice cream." She cocked her head to gesture to the cart across the street. "I'll just be a minute. What flavor would you like?"

She smiled enticingly and Adam's heart jumped in his chest.

"I'll have whatever you're having," he answered suavely.

With a devilish wink, she headed across the street and Adam settled down in the grass. Out of routine more than anything else, he pulled out his journal and started sketching Gene. The little boy needed no other playmates to entertain himself, and it wasn't long before he came across a new game—a duck.

With a strangely intent expression for one so young, he dropped into a crouch and began stealthily stalking the creature. Adam was riveted. Gene moved with undeniable grace, impressive for any age. His tiny muscles moved fluidly under his puffy toddler skin, and the look in his blue eyes could only be described as...primal.

Adam grabbed up his sketchpad and got to work. These were exactly the sort of differences he had been searching for. The slight distinction that let you know something was off. The pen flew of its own volition across the paper. In fact, Adam was so focused on his drawing that he jumped with surprise when he heard Lilly scream.

As if in slow motion, he saw her drop the ice cream cones and start running. Adam followed her gaze, and just as quickly discarded his sketchpad as he got up and sprinted towards the pond.

"Gene!" he gasped as he reached him. The boy's dark little head had just gone under.

Adam yanked him out of the water and dragged him onto the shore, checking his pulse and breathing as Lilly fell to her knees beside him. Gene twisted and giggled with all the attention, but Adam and Lilly were pale white.

"It was an accident, an accident," Adam kept repeating.

He stood a little ways off while Lilly ran her hands up and down Gene's wet little frame, checking for injuries. When she was satisfied, she turned on Adam.

"You didn't see him? What were you doing?!"

Adam glanced back at his notepad before saying once more. "It was an accident."

Infuriated, Lilly met his gaze and Adam sensed a chapter had closed.

"Come on, Gene." She took him by the hand and Adam trailed along behind as they went to get more ice cream.

***

Maren came to talk to Adam in his study that night.

"Lilly told me what happened," she said with no preface. "Adam, how could you?"

"It was an *accident*," he said for what seemed like the millionth time, hating himself, but trying to save face.

"But it's not just this one time," Maren hissed. "You never pay attention to him. You don't talk to him, you don't play with him. Hell, you talk about him as if he isn't even your *son*!"

Adam's eyes flashed. "That isn't true, Maren. I care about him very deeply."

"You care about him," she repeated. "You can't even say you *love* him!"

"How can you even suggest—?"

"No, that's it," she interrupted. "I've had enough."

Adam felt a chill run up his back. "What do you mean, you've had enough?"

"This has got to change. Adam, you can slight me, and insult me, and approach our relationship in your own insensitive way all you want. I fell in love with you just as you are. I knew what I was in for. But I am absolutely *not* going to watch you emotionally starve your own child."

Adam took quick, shallow breaths, willing himself to be calm. "So what are you saying?"

She brought herself up to her full height. "You're going to see a therapist."

Every ounce of Adam rebelled. "A therapist! Maren—"

"Let me rephrase," she said calmly. "You're going to see a therapist, or I'm leaving you."

The next day, Adam met with a therapist.

Maren had picked him out and scheduled the appointment, leaving Adam with the clear message that if he didn't show, he would not have a wife to come home to.

Adam shuffled his feet nervously as he waited for the man to arrive. Nowhere in last night's discussion had the word Asperger's come up, but he knew she'd been thinking it. On some level beneath the surface, it's what everyone was thinking the second he came into a room. Some days, he was thinking it himself.

The door opened behind his chair, and Adam got to his feet to introduce himself...

...to her?

Maren had picked a woman. How very disturbing. Adam was immediately on his guard. How could he discuss his feelings with a woman? It was bad enough that he was going to have to spend the entire session pretending she was a doctor in the same way that he was.

"Not what you were expecting?" she asked in a thick, German accent as she greeted him with a firm handshake.

Adam pulled himself together. "No—it's fine. I was just...I didn't realize you—"

"You thought I'd be a man," she surmised.

Adam flushed and glanced at the plaque above her desk. Christin Schulze. Could go either way. "Your name is surprisingly misleading."

She shrugged. "My parents thought I'd be a man as well. Shall we begin?"

"Of course." Adam rolled up his sleeves and took a seat, off-balance but rallying hard.

Dr. Schulze glanced down at her notes before fixing him squarely in her gaze. "So Adam, why are you here?"

The directness of the question threw him, and Adam hesitated a second before he replied.

"My two-year-old fell in a duck pond. While under my care."

The doctor nodded and wrote something down. "And you think you are the first parent to have such an accident? You decided to seek therapy because your child fell in a duck pond?"

"No," Adam clarified. "I'm here because my wife gave me an ultimatum."

"Ah, and she did this on a whim, did she? Didn't leave you...instead, she sent you to a place focused on self-betterment and healing. So I ask you again Adam, why are you here?"

He was starting to get a little angry now. Her tone wasn't exactly condescending, but the frank way in which she phrased her questions made him feel like his legs had been swept out from under him. He narrowed his eyes and answered somewhat icily.

"Maybe I should ask her."

Schulze looked at him over the rim of her glasses. "We can always schedule a group session, if that's what you'd like."

Truth be told, Adam could think of few things on the planet he would like less than that.

The question hung in the air between them until Adam was forced to break the silence.

"I have Asperger's."

"I see." For the first time her gaze softened, and she set down her pencil. "And you think that every single person with this syndrome seeks therapy? You think it's an automatic sentence for psychiatric care?"

"No, of course not!" Adam countered, trying not to raise his voice. "There may be certain idiosyncrasies implied with the word, but I don't believe it has the power to stop any individual from being a happy and productive member of society."

"I agree." She leaned back in her chair and regarded him thoughtfully. "So I ask you again; Adam, *why are you here?*"

Adam gulped. She may be a doctor after all.

Chapter 11

Now that the world knew Adam's name, it was necessary to protect what he'd done.

In order to patent the vaccine, all Adam's sources would have to be revealed. That meant the donor. But unless Adam wanted to be charged with desecration of a corpse, falsification of Gene's parentage, and so on and so forth, he would be keeping that little detail to himself.

But the process itself could be patented, and Adam was quick to secure it to his name.

The preliminary results from the Mexican clinics had astounded everyone; reports indicated that most cancers had shriveled and disappeared after the third injection. A photographer from Time Magazine was deployed, and once again, the press was at Adam's door.

It was a little easier to evade tricky questions from the press since the work had been done in Mexico. However, a handful of the world's leading drug companies had gotten into the game and were asking how to mass produce the vaccine. After a hasty discussion with Maren, Adam decided that they needed to go down in person and visit the clinics.

The final results had been made available to him, but the details involved in the individual case studies were still a mystery.

Leaving Gene safely in Lilly's capable hands, Adam and Maren took off on the first flight from SFO to Mexico City. There, they would travel from clinic to clinic to see precisely where their trial stood. Most of the information would simply be taken back home with them for analysis, but patient interviews and clinic observation had to be done in person. They'd given themselves twenty days to see seven different clinics, so from the moment they landed, they were on the go.

"I still think we should have seen the clinics in the capital first," Adam complained as they piled into the back of a cab and headed to Azurobo.

Maren pulled her hair back into a messy bun and cracked the window for some air. "I told you, they asked for a few more days to organize their data when they learned you were coming in person. I think you make them nervous."

"That's ridiculous!" Adam threw up his hands. "How would I possibly make anyone nervous?"

Maren rolled her eyes. "You're right. You appear to be a pillar of stability."

"I'm serious, Maren. We're not taking any slack from these people. They should be organized enough already and if they're not...why are we stopping?"

They looked out the window as their car rolled to a gentle stop on a deserted street.

Maren frowned. "I don't—"

"*Get down!*"

Shards of glass rained over their heads as the windows of the cab were smashed by two men wielding knives. Maren screamed and grabbed onto Adam as the men jumped in on either side of them and locked the doors.

"Don't move!"

Adam cringed and held Maren tight against his chest as one of the men screamed in his ear.

"Close your eyes, put your heads down, and empty your pockets."

They spoke in perfect English, and Adam got the sense they had done this many times before.

"Lady — give me your purse."

In less than a minute, Adam and Maren were stripped of all their credit cards, cash, phones, and jewelry. For good measure, they were even made to surrender their passports. They clung to each other for support as they were searched and said not a word, each one praying that the men would be satisfied and stop with that.

"What about this?"

Maren shrieked as one of the men grabbed her wrist and held out her hand. The other one looked at her impassively and nodded his head. "Take it."

"*No*," she whimpered as he forced open her fingers and pulled off her wedding ring.

Adam held her even tighter. "Quiet," he whispered, eying the blade pressed threateningly against his stomach. "It's just a ring."

One of the bandits grinned, exposing multiple gold teeth. "That's right, lady. Just a ring. You should be happy we aren't looking for anything else."

He looked her up and down in a way that made Adam's blood boil, and he literally had to bite down on his lips to keep from exploding.

"Now drive!"

The next hour was the longest of Adam and Maren's lives. They kept their heads down between their knees as the thieves made the cabbie drive around in circles. Silent tears pooled in a puddle at Maren's feet. Perhaps the most terrifying thing was that the men didn't wear masks. It was as if they were so sure of themselves that they didn't care if anyone could identify them. It made the couple shudder as to what exactly they intended to do.

But the nightmare passed.

With no warning, the car stopped again and Adam and Maren were released. They gasped and held each other in the middle of the road, watching the taxi grow smaller and smaller in the distance. Right before it disappeared altogether, a hand poked out and waved.

Maren threw up. Adam patted her back and looked helplessly around them. They were unharmed, yes, but the bandits had left them in the middle of a sinister neighborhood with no phones, and no money to get home.

"It's okay, it's okay," he calmed her and held back her hair until she was finished. When she straightened up, he put his hands on the side of her face and studied her carefully. "Are you okay? Are you still with me?"

She gave a shaky nod and wiped her mouth on her sleeve. Her eyes were still red from the crying, and as she looked around the desolate neighborhood, she crossed her arms protectively across her chest. "What are we going to do?"

It was one of the few moments in their relationship Maren could look back and say that Adam really came through for her.

He took her hand with a gentle smile and gestured up the road. "Now, my dear, we walk."

They trudged up the dirt road for the next four hours, following cracked street signs, and asking in broken Spanish if they were nearing Azurobo. About two hours in, there was a snapping sound as one of Maren's heels broke. Pursing her lips, she took them off and they continued in silence. The sun went down and the stars came out, bringing with them the slightly ominous sounds of night. Stray dogs and an occasional homeless person would follow them for a bit before losing interest and moving on. At one point, they could swear they heard gunfire.

When they finally saw the lights in the distance they picked up their pace, and were practically jogging by the time they reached the safety of the town. There was only one place to stay in the entire city, but even though their luggage was already there waiting for them, without any money or identification, they were unable to claim it or secure even basic accommodations.

After over an hour of negotiation, partially because of Adam's incessant rambling and mostly because Maren started silently crying, the concierge finally conceded and gave them the cheapest room of the lot. While it was being prepared, Adam commandeered the phone at the front desk and contacted the United States Consulate. With their assistance, banks were contacted, money was wired, and new credit cards and passports were issued to be sent overnight by FedEx.

"Did you hear that?" Adam asked the hotel's manager. "We can pay for all of this in four hours when the transfer comes through."

The manager looked at him skeptically, but handed him a key to a room on the first floor with a wry smile. "Enjoy your stay."

Ten minutes later, they were finally alone.

"This is nice," Maren said with dulled sarcasm, running her hand over the comforter before thinking better of it and pulling it back.

"It's quiet," Adam said thoughtfully, staring up at the ceiling fan. "I miss the quiet."

Maren gave him a long look, then went to explore the bathroom. She emerged a moment later looking almost as shaken as she had in the cab.

"I'm ready to go home," she murmured, thinking of Gene.

"Me too," Adam agreed, imagining his peaceful lab. "I'm ready to go back."

Both of them lay on top of their coats on the made-up bed that night. Both unaware of what the other was thinking. Both feeling strangely alone.

Maren was already up the next morning when Adam opened his eyes. He propped himself up on his elbows and stretched groggily as she came into the room holding a FedEx package and two paper cups of steaming hot coffee.

"This came." She tossed the thick envelope onto the bed beside him.

Sure enough, inside were two new passports and a small array of credit cards. Adam inspected them meticulously before slipping them inside his wallet. It was amazing how naked he'd felt without basic modern conveniences. Adam felt safer already just knowing they were there.

"Did everything come through okay?" Maren asked.

Adam looked up with concern. Her voice was scratchy and rough, and her hands jerked disjointedly as she tried to add sugar and cream.

They may have escaped unharmed, but they were not leaving Mexico without some scars.

"Hey, come here," he said, holding open his arms.

After a slight pause, she set down her cup and nestled down beside him, laying her head against his slowly beating heart. He stroked her hair again and again until she eventually relaxed in the steady rhythm and calmed down.

"I was so scared," she whispered.

Adam sighed. "I know. I was too."

Her eyes clouded up as she stared vacantly at the broken television. "It's like, we have this amazing life, and I don't take any of it for granted, but then something like that happens and you realize...." Her voice choked up and she stifled a sob.

Adam resumed his gentle caress and kissed the top of her head. His mind travelled back to Italy, to the start of his journey. To the fortuitous series of events that led him to this very moment, poised to go down in scientific history as one of the greatest geneticists that ever lived.

He couldn't imagine losing such a thing when it was so close.

"I want to hold Gene. I want to sleep in my bed with my husband. I want to have all my family back together again."

Maren sniffed and leaned back so she could see his face.

"It really makes you clarify your priorities, you know?"

Adam briefly met her eyes before pulling her back to his chest.

"Yes. I guess it does."

Chapter 12

After a few days back in Berkeley, the Mexican nightmare seemed like a distant memory. The Christmas season was upon them and little Gene was flush with excitement. In fact, there seemed to be very little that didn't excite Gene these days. From the second that Adam and Maren walked in the door, he bombarded them with breaking news about his preschool, his friends, his nanny Lilly, giraffes, the zoo, and even the Santa exhibit at the mall.

No detail was too small to get lost in the recounting.

Adam listened to the monologue with strained patience, but Maren seemed physically unable to let Gene go. Ever since their harrowing encounter she'd developed a strong fixation on family, and the way she was stroking Gene's hair as he babbled on about reindeer made Adam nervous.

When Maren finally announced it was bedtime and they tucked Gene safely away to sleep, Adam felt as though he could still hear echoes of the little, chirping voice. He squeezed his eyes tightly shut and grabbed himself an Advil from the bathroom cabinet as Maren slipped in behind him.

"He missed you so much. Look how excited he was to tell you everything that you missed." She smiled contentedly and wrapped her arms around Adam's back. "It's so good to be home."

He reached around her to swallow the pill. "It sure is."

The next morning Maren stayed home with Gene, while Lilly and Adam split off to do a little holiday shopping. Gene's list of demands this year had been extensive, and each of them had a specific shopping directive. Yet they somehow ended up in very different places.

Lilly bought a G.I. Joe and a Tickle-Me-Elmo.

Adam bought a gun.

He hadn't planned on doing it. In fact, he hadn't even realized where his aimless driving was taking him until he was parked in front of the shop.

As a general rule, Adam didn't approve of guns. He had never considered getting one, and was quite surprised himself when he ended up buying a small caliber revolver. But his experience in Mexico had changed him in a way he was only beginning to understand.

He would not sit by as a helpless victim while others forced their will upon him. He would never again lose that kind of control.

He also decided that he wouldn't tell anyone.

He wasn't sure if Maren would approve of having a gun in the house, and he didn't feel like having the argument if she was opposed. Instead, he placed it inside the center drawer of his desk, the thin one he never used, and hoped to never think of it again.

Gene's Christmas presents were a huge success. He was especially taken with the Tickle-Me-Elmo. When squeezed, Elmo would chortle. When squeezed three times in a row, Elmo would begin to shake and laugh hysterically. When squeezed more times than that, Gene's parents would think of ways to discreetly murder Elmo.

After presents the little family headed to the zoo, where a display had been created with elves, and reindeer, and even a small hill of real snow for the kids to play in. No one could play harder than Gene. Despite being a bit younger than most of the kids around him, he took up the position of "captain" of the sled, and fearlessly flew through the flurries again and again.

When he'd finally had his fill, the tired couple headed back home for Christmas dinner. They'd invited both Lilly and Kendra to dine with them, and although Kendra had flown home to be with her family, Lilly gratefully took them up on their offer.

It turned out to be a little more awkward than anyone had foreseen.

Lilly sat at one end of the table, Adam on the other, and Maren placed herself squarely in between them. They chatted nervously and made idle small talk, until Adam wisely steered the conversation towards how Gene was adjusting to preschool.

"Oh, he's amazing!" Lilly glowed. "When I picked him up the day before winter vacation, his teacher told me that he had 'unusually high intelligence' and was one of the fastest learners in the class."

"Of course he is." Maren heaped another spoonful of Christmas pudding onto Gene's plate and he gobbled it down. "Just look who his father is."

Adam held it together through the holidays, but the day after New Year's he was back in the office. The remaining clinics they hadn't visited in Mexico had very kindly sent over detailed reports of their case studies for Maren and Adam to review at home, and while there were a few cases where the cancer had already caused too much damage for the host body to respond, in over ninety percent of the cases, the serum proved effective.

Several drug companies began courting Adam for his patent. It was time to go public and get the vaccine into production. Between the African and Mexican trials, the results had proven effective enough that the companies themselves volunteered to put the vaccine into further trials, and since the process had been patented, Adam would be able to sell the raw material — tiny amounts of Gene's blood — to the various groups for cloning purposes. As long as the companies accepted these terms and conditions, Adam was on his way to becoming a multi-millionaire.

But the more he thought about it, the more he didn't relish the idea of any facet of the trial getting away from him. After all, he had begun the study himself; brought it from the highest reaches of the Italian Alps, to the jungle villages of India, from Africa to Mexico, and now to his home in Berkeley. It was his; controlled in his very own study. He didn't want to surrender it.

He didn't want to lose control.

Instead, he decided to form his own company. He needed to borrow huge sums of money to get it started, but the future was a golden one with the promise of the miracle vaccine. A new lifestyle was in order, and before long, he and Maren found themselves victory shopping for cars.

Maren settled on a Volvo station wagon, Platinum Edition. The perfect vehicle to enhance her carefully crafted image of the "Berkeley suburban mom." Adam, on the other hand, went sailing off to therapy in a shiny new Porsche 911. He'd dropped Lilly off on the way there.

It seemed a ride in a Porsche could undo a fall in a pond.

He saw the blinds twitch in Dr. Schulze's office as he came screeching to a stop in the parking lot. Uh-oh. He wondered what Freud would have to say about this.

"Good evening," he greeted her as he swept into the room and took a seat on the couch.

She lowered her glasses. "Good evening. You're in a fine mood today."

Adam smiled. "Well, things have been going well for me lately."

"Yes, how so?"

The smile faltered. "Don't you watch the news?"

"Let's assume I don't," she answered dryly.

Adam traced the designs in the carpet with his shoe. Where should he even begin?

"I created my own company to sell my 'mirac—" He hastily caught himself. "My vaccine. It's starting to turn quite a profit."

The doctor nodded and scribbled something down. "And how has that been for your family? Adjusting to the change?"

Adam paused, mind scrambling to understand. "What do you mean?"

Schulze took off her glasses and put them on her desk. "Adam, what did we decide we would be attempting here?"

"Cognitive behavioral therapy."

"That's right. Cognitive behavioral therapy. Understanding the emotions of the people around you. Making connections."

Adam's mind flashed back to Lilly and the Porsche.

"I have connections."

The doctor shook her head. "But you don't understand them, treat them as individuals. You're not sensitive to their nuanced emotional state, and as such, it's impossible for you to produce an appropriate reaction."

Adam leaned back on the sofa. "Impossible, huh. Then what have we been doing here these last few weeks?"

Schulze sighed. "Adam, we can play word games if you wish, but you know I'll win."

There was an unfortunate air of truth to that.

Adam relaxed his posture and settled back against the cushions. "I am trying. When Maren and I were attacked in Mexico, I bent over backwards to comfort her. On Christmas we took Gene to the zoo so he could play in the snow."

...I bought a gun.

Adam decided to leave that part out.

"And how did Gene like the snow?" she asked encouragingly.

Adam brightened at this. "He took to it much better than the other children. He was the fastest one to climb back up the hill, and he had no trouble navigating the sled back down again."

Schulze stared at him. "I see."

Adam flushed. "What do you want me to say?"

"How did it make Gene feel?"

"You'd have to ask him, Doctor."

But she didn't give an inch of ground. "As your therapist, I'm asking you. This is exactly the sort of thing we're talking about, Adam. You're his parent—his father. Especially at this age, you should have a pretty good idea of what's going on in his head."

Adam was silent for a long while.

"He was laughing," he finally said. "He was enjoying himself; it made him happy."

She nodded. "That's good. And did seeing Gene enjoy himself make you want to take him back there again, to see him so happy?"

Adam frowned. "It honestly hadn't occurred to me."

"That, Adam, is the bulk of our problem."

A rush of emotions boiled just under his skin. He'd actually started to appreciate their weekly talks, but who was this woman to be telling him about his problems? She wasn't perfect herself.

"I'm an obsessive compulsive acrophobe with an intense, irrational fear of sharks."

Adam froze in stunned silence as she continued writing. When she was finished, she looked up with a grim smile.

"I've seen that look on the face of many patients before you."

He processed this for a second before asking, "So what would you have me do?"

"Focus on yourself right now. I know your work is taking you to new heights, but every time I see you, Adam, you seem more agitated than the last. You need stability right now. A return to normalcy. Once you get your center back, we can worry about how you relate to other people."

Adam nodded in compliance; all this made sense.

"No more trips to Mexico. No sudden sports cars. Just try to keep things on an even keel."

The drive back home was much slower than the one to the office, and Adam made sure to obey all the traffic laws. Dr. Schulze was right. Ever since his sabbatical, his life had been spiraling out of control. Now that he had a drug trial and a family that depended on him, he would need that control more than ever.

He pulled slowly into the driveway and replayed the mantra in his head.

A return to normalcy. No more surprises. Keeping things on an even keel.

He could do that. He could find stability in routine. He would be better for it, and in the end, his family would be better for it too. He just needed to find his old rhythm again.

When he pushed open the door, Maren was waiting on the base of the stairs. One look at her face told him that something was happening, and he stopped dead in his tracks.

"Maren, what is it? What's wrong?"

She gave him a long look, her face betraying no emotion.

"I'm pregnant."

Chapter 13

"Oh God — Adam, you look like you should sit down. Do you want to sit down? We could move to the sofa...I could get you some water. You really should sit."

As the walls closed in around him, Adam slid to the floor against the front door. His shirt hiked up behind him and the cool wood pressed against his back helped steady his nerves.

"There." His voice was barely audible. "Sitting."

Maren watched him with wide eyes, trying to determine his next move. When nothing happened for a minute or two, she shifted her weight nervously and cleared her throat. Adam's eyes slowly lifted from the entryway tiles and settled on her face.

"Are you sure?"

She spoke in a rush of air, eager to get everything out in the open now that he knew. "Positive. I went to the obstetrician earlier today...the baby's due in August."

Adam tried to do some quick, mental math, but for the first time ever, his brilliant mind failed him. Instead, he gazed helplessly at Maren, grasping wildly for a life raft.

"But…how did this happen? I thought you were on the pill."

Maren's face flushed incriminatingly. "I am — um, I was. Dr. Dufor told me that there's a certain percentage of failure with the pill."

Adam looked distant and remote. "…and this is that failure."

Cautious but incensed, Maren rallied, "This is our *baby*. It's not a failure."

Adam looked up with feeling, but something about Maren's face stopped him from suggesting an abortion. The stability she provided to the family was keeping them afloat, and he had been afraid something like this would happen ever since Mexico. They each had their own way of coping.

Adam got a gun. Maren got a baby.

And the profound distinction between men and women was made painfully clear.

"Gene will be better for having a sibling."

Adam glanced up with dulled hope. A silver lining? He supposed it was true. It could only enhance Adam's study, from an anthropological standpoint, to see how Gene would react to a change in family dynamics. But his orderly mind flailed in the chaos, and he took a few deep breaths as he tried to fit this new piece of information into his carefully structured world.

Keep things on an even keel. If Schulze could see him now.

"So," his brow furrowed in concentration, "I guess this means…."

Maren knelt in front of him and took his hand. "This means, we're having a baby."

And just like that, things changed.

The next few months flew by in a blur.

Maren's pregnancy progressed well through the mild Berkeley summer, and Adam spent more time than ever sneaking off by himself. His dalliances and infidelities expanded from just Lilly to a wider circle, and while Adam felt almost sure that on a certain level Maren had to know, his increasing prestige seemed to balance it out.

And what prestige it was!

His vaccine continued to save countless lives on every continent. He was in demand as a speaker as well as an author, promoting a memoir he'd written about the early trials. A movie deal was in the works, and there were even whispers of a Nobel Prize for Medicine and Physiology for his outstanding contribution to the peoples of the world.

It seemed as though no one could touch him. His massive web of deception and lies had somehow come together to build the very foundations of a life he could not have even imagined. The world was at his fingertips, and he was set to go down in history as one of the greats, just as he'd planned.

But despite his every success, Adam could never feel truly happy. He'd done too much, lied too much, crossed too far over the line. Eventually, something had to break. A straw house was not made to last forever.

One little crack, one little chip in the façade...and the whole thing could go up in flames.

He and Dr. Schulze danced around this issue in therapy. She was an incredibly astute woman, skilled at her craft, and while she realized his ever-changing world of different people and places wasn't exactly copasetic for a man of his condition, she had still found nothing to account for his chronic feeling of unease and inability to take joy in his triumphs.

Of course, Adam knew the reason. In fact, he'd been thinking about his Otzi indiscretion more and more these last few months. He blamed it on the coming baby — it gave everything that "clock's ticking" impending feeling of doom, and forced him to look back on his life in judgment. But with inadvertent help from Dr. Schulze, he'd recently made a breakthrough.

He no longer believed he had done anything wrong.

By ethical standards — yes. And the scientific community was sure to think so if they ever found out. But in an international, historical context? No — he didn't believe he had.

Would the world rather he hadn't disturbed a five-thousand year old dead man and left his body alone? Would they rather he hadn't created Gene and made the vaccine that had already saved thousands of lives?

It would go on to save millions. The entire continent of Africa would be given a chance to rise from the ashes of HIV and give life to another generation to carry on their legacy. Every person with cancer who'd ever been handed a death sentence now had a chance to live. The effect this one tiny vaccine would have on the planet was staggering.

And Otzi? What did he lose? Well, Adam knew first hand it was nothing he would miss.

That left the question of Gene himself.

If he were to ever learn the truth, how could he be angry? If Adam hadn't acted as he had, Gene would never have been born. He'd have remained a frozen impossibility, forever on display in some museum as the people around him slowly deteriorated and died, not knowing the key to their very survival was looking at them, trapped behind the glass.

Sometimes in his musings, Adam got a little carried away.

Regardless, he had effectively excused himself from any and all blame. If the world were to somehow reveal his mighty secret, so be it. Let them come. They could find nothing to charge him with that his medical contribution hadn't far outweighed.

That being said, he was determined to take the secret to his grave.

But in order for there to be a vaccine at all, there would have to be blood, and Adam was having a harder and harder time getting a sample from Gene. Not only did the little boy cry for one of his female protectors whenever his father was left alone with him, but he wriggled and fought so much when Adam tried to take a sample from his heel that Adam had actually ended up accidentally hurting him several times.

It was on one of these days that Maren heard Gene wailing and wandered inside from the garden. When she came upon Adam holding the child, who was bleeding excessively from the foot, she stopped dead in her tracks.

"What are you doing?" she asked in a low voice.

Adam froze. Shouldn't she be asking "What happened" rather than "What have you done?"

Collecting his wits, he lifted Gene up even higher and looked down at the floor. "He stepped on a nail or a thumb tack or something. I can't find it."

It was the wrong thing to say to a pregnant woman.

What followed was a vigorous baby-proofing and cleaning regimen that was only finally ruled complete when little Sophie came into the world on August 19, 1997. She did so by tub, as did many children of the avant garde women of Berkeley, leaving Gene with the confused impression that his new sister must be a mermaid.

"What do you think, Gene?" Maren asked with a smile after Sophie was cleaned up and sleeping in a swaddled blanket. "Do you want to hold your new sister?"

Gene had been obsessed with placing his hands on Maren's stomach all summer long to feel "his baby," but now that the moment of truth was upon him, he was suddenly shy.

"I don't know...." He backed away into Lilly's legs for comfort.

"Come on, it'll be okay," Maren insisted, holding out the baby. "Lilly will help you. You just put one hand under her back, and another up to support her head."

The two women situated the baby in Gene's rigid arms, and smiled as he looked worriedly down at her reddish face.

"That's good, little man!" Lilly encouraged. "You're doing a great job!"

Gene frowned as he looked between his sister and the birthing tub. "I don't think she can breathe above the water," he whispered.

Adam was quick to drain the tub before any life-saving heroics on Gene's part accidently drowned his sister, and together, over the next few days, the little family settled in with its newest member.

Kendra moved back into the household part time to help with Sophie, and it soon became clear that the Barfields had grown out of their current residence. A frantic house hunt commenced, and after finding a realtor whose husband had used Adam's vaccine to cure his colon cancer, they soon found themselves looking at a lovely home higher up in the Berkeley Hills.

Even with all the extra help they hired the move was an ordeal, an effort made no easier by Gene's aggressive insistence that he was in charge of the baby for the move.

Little Sophie, or "Sissie," as Gene preferred to call her, was under his care, and he delighted in preemptively challenging anyone who might dare suggest otherwise.

While the adults might have found Gene's protective instincts adorable on any other day, when the time came to drive away from their old house forever, they seriously considered leaving him.

With the new house came more rooms, more square-footage, and an ample yard. While the adults wandered around inside, staking claims in terms of offices and closet space, Gene decided to set up outside in back beneath the large oak tree. There was plenty of room, and for now, no one had noticed he'd taken his favorite blanket and pillow and had resolved to stay. But the enclosed yard was too big for just one little boy, and before long, Gene had hatched a plan.

"My friend Cameron has a dog," he complained for the umpteenth time at dinner. "Cameron's dog is his very best friend in the world."

"Well, that doesn't say a lot for Cameron then." Maren scooped green beans onto his plate. "Eat your vegetables."

"But I would love it, and be so careful with it, and feed it, and give it toys, and it could sleep in my room, and...." His little mind raced and he came up with an exasperated sigh. "I need someone to help me take care of Sophie."

Adam and Maren exchanged a glance and tried very hard to keep from laughing. Oh, the endless toils of a five-year-old father.

Gene's campaign had been hard fought, and the next day, Adam and Maren went out to a shelter to find him a dog. Only, it turned out they had very different ideas of what "dog" meant.

"Oh my God, Adam, she's *perfect!*"

Maren held the little puff ball against her face, and after a moment, Adam realized it was actually a living thing.

He wrinkled up his nose. "We can't get that, it looks like a cotton ball. I thought you were using it to powder your face." He strolled up and down the aisles and came to a stop in front of a powerful looking German shepherd. "No…this is what Gene needs. A real dog."

Maren joined him and looked at the animal in horror. "What? So it could eat him after it's done playing with him? That thing's enormous, Adam!"

"It's a protector," he countered, pointing to the little sign on the wall of the cage. "It says German shepherds are fiercely loyal to their families, and that this one's been waiting here for four months…for someone like *you*, Maren."

He made a pleading face to rival that of Gene, and Maren burst out into giggles. She rarely saw this playful side of him, and was all the more besotted.

"Well…," she smiled, "I'm sure we can come to some sort of arrangement."

"Two dogs!"

Gene was absolutely beside himself with excitement. He stood frozen in between them, palsied into immobility by the frantic joy in his little heart.

"Thank you, thank you, thank you!"

He leapt first on Maren, and then on Adam as he squeezed them tightly in gratitude. Adam was a little taken aback; he could probably count on one hand the number of times Gene had embraced him like this, and he froze awkwardly before gently unwinding the little boy's finger

"Why don't you go play with them?" he suggested.

Gene's eyes whirled around to his new companions and his little fingers curled in glee. "What are their names?" he asked excitedly.

Maren grinned. "That's up to you. Do you have any ideas?"

"Dazzle and Tousel," he said with absolutely no hesitation.

Again, Maren and Adam shared a bewildered look, but this time, Maren threw up her hands with a smile and headed into the kitchen. "He's all yours."

The dogs had been a wonderful addition to the family. The shepherd, Dazzle, absolutely loved Gene and guarded him with adoration. Tousel, the little puff ball, was incredibly playful herself, and ran as fast as her pint-size legs would carry her as the three of them raced around the yard.

It was a picturesque scene, but Adam was rarely there to see it. As the millennium came and passed, he spent more and more time away in his office at the university. When he was home, he continued to take endless secretive notes on Gene.

He was a perfect boy.

There was nothing at all unusual in his appearance for anyone to suspect that he wasn't just another Californian Caucasian. His dark blue eyes were steady and clear, and as the years progressed and he grew older, he had started developing strong feelings of right and wrong. He had been at the top of his class every year since he'd started, he deeply cherished his little sister, and to everyone else, he was charming and kind.

A perfect boy.

That was…until the accident.

Chapter 14

In hindsight, Adam and Maren felt like they should have seen it coming.

Every day when he returned home from school, Gene would race outside and spend endless hours playing with Sophie and the two dogs. They romped and ran, threw sticks and fetched Frisbees, laughed and screamed, and lived in a carefree, Utopian bubble.

But Maren and Adam were not the only ones to have noticed. The two neglected pit bulls on the other side of the fence had built up a slush fund of resentment towards the happy family next door, and one day in the summer of 2001, all that pent up aggression came to a head.

Sophie was four and Gene was just nine when the pit bulls jumped over the fence and into the Barfield's yard. It was pandemonium. The two dogs attacked with all the ferocity inbred into their kind, launching themselves at the helpless little ones and their protectors. Soon, Tousel was just a bloody mop on the grass. No sign of life issued from her tiny body. Dazzle fought with all her stout heart and beautiful soul, but she was no match for the deadly, killing machines. After a vicious struggle, she fell to the grass, finally succumbing to the loss of blood and coordination.

That only left little Gene to defend his precious Sissie.

He grabbed a stick and began beating at the heads of the pit bulls, trying to poke them in the eyes. But the pit bulls had only one function: kill. By the time Lilly heard the noise from inside, the damage had been done.

Dazzle was lying in a pool of her own blood, and Tousel would never breathe again. Thanks to the sacrifices of her brother and their loyal dogs, Sophie was curled up in a tiny fetal position, but was unharmed. Gene was another story.

"Oh my God! *Gene!*" Lilly screamed as she tore out of the kitchen.

He was lying beneath the oak tree, bleeding profusely from several severe slashes that had shredded his skin and clothes. The pit bulls had torn into his wrists where he had tried to protect himself, and into his neck where they had tried to kill him. He was alive...but barely.

Keeping one hand on both children, Lilly whirled around and picked up the stick herself. But she needn't have bothered. Hesitant and cowering now that an adult had arrived, the pit bulls made yet another great escape and returned to their yard.

Sophie clung to Lilly's shirt as she picked up Gene and ran him inside. With trembling fingers, she dialed 911, and a few minutes later an ambulance arrived. The paramedics put Gene on life support and loaded him up into the cab, while Lilly tried to get a hold of Maren and Adam, piling Sophie into her car as they followed the ambulance to the hospital.

***

"What do you mean, *accident*?!" Adam yelled into the receiver, pulling on his jacket and sprinting past his bewildered students through the lab.

"Those two pit bulls next door got over the fence! He's on life support, Adam—you need to get here now! They're trying to match his blood for a transfusion."

Adam's face whitened as he hung up the phone and jumped into his car. There were a total of thirty human blood groupings currently recognized by the International Society of Blood Transfusion. Over six-hundred sub-variations had been found to account for specific ethnic groups, and now every human being on the planet would fall into one of these divisions.

But Gene wouldn't.

Adam drove faster, and soon the towering walls of Alta Bates came into view. He parked in the emergency loading zone and raced into the lobby just as Maren was reaching the nurses' station. Her eyes were red and swollen, and she saw Adam, she erupted into a fresh fit of tears.

"I can't believe this is happening!" she sobbed. "They won't even let me up to see him; he's in the operating room now!"

"Where's Lilly and the baby?" Adam demanded, waves of testosterone-fueled adrenaline coursing through his veins.

"They're in the lobby—Sophie's fine." She tried to pull herself together. "Adam, they said something about wanting to test our blood. They're trying to do a transfusion...." Her voice trailed off and she stifled another sob. "I told them I wasn't his biological mother. Adam—what blood type is he?"

But Adam was already gone, running full-tilt to the ICU. He pushed through the Personnel Only doors and burst in on a room full of doctors hovering over his fallen son. When Adam saw Gene's lifeless body, all the fight seemed to go out of him. He half-collapsed against the wall, and didn't realize what was happening until one of the doctors had removed him into the hall.

"Sir?"

The man's mouth was moving, but the sound was distorted and far away. Adam focused on his lips as he shook his head, trying to get control of himself.

"Sir," the doctor said again, "is that your son?"

"Yes," Adam panted, finally coming round. "Yes, that's my son."

Why hadn't he said the words more often? Why hadn't he said them to Gene?

The doctor nodded brusquely, "We're going to need to give you a blood test — we're trying to arrange a transfusion. For some reason, he isn't coming up as a match to anything in our computers."

"Of course you can test me, of course," Adam said, holding out his arm on the spot.

But even as he rolled up his sleeve, he knew it would be no use. He wasn't any more connected to Gene than the man sticking the syringe in his arm.

Another doctor came out to check on them, and Adam peeled himself slowly off the wall. "His mother — his biological mother — was a surrogate in a remote village in India. If Gene's not a match to any groupings you have, that's probably why."

The doctors looked at him with interest, accepting this explanation on the spot as there were no others to compare it to. The first physician disappeared inside with a vial of Adam's blood, while the second stayed out to comfort him.

"Well, we'll test you regardless, and if not, we're going to need your permission to try transfusing with the universal blood donor. I must confess, Mr. Barfield, it's a risky move; his body could easily reject the transfusion. But the fact remains—your son needs blood. I don't see what other choice we have."

Adam nodded hastily. "No, you're right, it's the only option. I'll sign whatever you need me to."

For the next four hours the little Barfield family huddled together in the waiting room, craning their necks every time a doctor walked past, hoping it was someone coming to tell them about Gene. Sophie had curled up on Maren's lap and cried herself to sleep, and Lilly's shirt was still covered in Gene's blood, so she had gone home to change.

Adam and Maren held hands, but didn't say a word. There was nothing left to say.

The door opened and they looked up quickly, only to see Kendra slip inside. The second she saw the two of them and little Sophie, she started silently weeping. Maren squeezed Adam's hand as a signal, and he got up and gave her a comforting hug.

"I just can't believe it!" she cried. "Lilly called me on her way back to your house. Have they told you anything new? Is Sophie okay?"

"No, they haven't told us anything new; they're transfusing him as we speak." Adam sat her down in the chair across from them.

In a way, it was a good thing that it was taking so long for an update. It meant that his body hadn't immediately rejected the blood. Adam imagined they were monitoring him very closely before coming to a conclusive opinion as to the transfusion's success.

"Maren, honey, can I get you anything?" Kendra offered. "Do you want me to go down to the cafeteria and get everyone some snacks or coffee? Maybe some juice for Sophie?"

Maren forced a tight smile. "That would be nice, Kendra. Thank you." Her phone buzzed and she shifted Sophie on her hip so she could check her text message. "Lilly says that the Hesses next door had no idea what had happened; the dogs were already back in their yard." She bit her lip suddenly and sniffed. "She also said Dazzle died."

There was a quiet moment of silence to honor their fallen hero.

"If those dogs aren't gone by the time we get back, I'm going to kill them myself," Adam growled.

Just then the door pushed open and an exhausted-looking surgeon came inside, followed immediately by another doctor in different colored scrubs. Adam and Maren stood up of one accord.

"What happened? How is he?" Maren demanded, still biting her lip to keep calm.

"The transfusion went very well," the surgeon assured them. "The critical period for rejection has passed and he appears to be accepting the blood. That being said, we still want to watch him very closely."

Adam and Maren grabbed each other in silent relief, crushing Sophie in between them.

"His lacerations are a different story…."

The door opened again and Kendra came inside, holding stacks of sandwiches and coffee. She stared at the doctors, holding her breath, until Maren gave her a reassuring nod and put Sophie in her waiting arms.

"He's going to be okay. Can you watch her outside while we talk to the doctor?"

"Of course!" she exhaled. "That's so good to hear!"

Kendra and Sophie disappeared outside and the rest of them sat down.

***

"We had to give him over two-hundred stitches just to get the wounds mostly closed, but he's not out of the woods yet. Most of the worst lesions were on his neck, and in dog bites, we often see a deep tissue injury that doesn't manifest itself for a couple of days." He paused and stared back into the wide eyes of the terrified couple. "Are you guys with me so far?"

Maren was unable to speak, but Adam gripped her firmly and nodded. "We understand the severity, please go on."

"He's going to need skin grafts, first artificial, and then from samples we can take from his own body. I'm not going to lie to you, he's in pretty bad shape. But that being said, I've seen worse cases than his before, and those children have gone on to make a perfectly healthy recovery with relatively little scarring."

Maren took a deep breath. "But he's going to be fine?" Her voice shook and she squeezed Adam's hand harder. "I mean...we're not going to...lose him?"

The doctor shook his head and smiled. "No, Mrs. Barfield. Your friend called the ambulance in the nick of time. With a bit of work, I anticipate a full physical recovery."

Right now, Maren would give Lilly just about anything. She was on the verge of forgiving her for sleeping with her husband. In fact, she was considering making her a medal.

But the doctor wasn't finished.

"But that's just the physical. Psychologically, it's a whole other story. That's where my colleague comes in."

The second man reached forward with a professional smile and shook both of their hands. "I'm Dr. Gelson...I'm in charge of your son's case. Now I know this is sudden, but I wanted to give you a brief consult about what we're in for before Gene wakes up. Attacks like this tend to leave psychosocial scars just as deep as the cuts themselves. Gene went through an incredibly traumatic experience, and he's going to need help to resolve those issues."

Maren started nodding quickly, pulling out a pen and paper to take notes. "Yes, of course. What would you recommend?"

"Well, first off, how's his support network? Is it just the three of you in the house?"

"No," Adam responded, "we also have a live-in nurse and a nanny."

The doctor nodded. "What about friends? Teachers? Is there anyone he'd latched onto especially tight that could help?"

Adam and Maren racked their brains but came up blank.

"Not really," she answered. "The thing he really latched onto the hardest was…." Her eyes fell and she looked down at her phone. "He loved our dogs."

Adam squeezed her knee and the surgeon nodded understandingly. "Well, I'm not a psychologist, but if it were me, I'd hold off on getting him any new pets for a while. That's going to be an emotional landmine."

They agreed and Maren waved for Kendra and Sophie to come in. She needed to hold her other baby right now. The doctors scooted over to make room for the girls.

"Well, I can see that Gene certainly has plenty of female companionship in his life." The psychologist smiled at Sophie.

"Yes," Adam rolled his eyes good-naturedly, "it's a bit of an estrogen fest. I think even his teacher is a woman."

"Well, what about male role models? You never know what kind of figure a child is going to need to comfort themselves. Are you the only man Gene has regular contact with?"

"Um, yes, I suppose it would just be me."

The doctor nodded. "And how's your relationship?"

Adam stiffened. "How do you mean?"

He looked up over his chart. "Can he come to you? Are you usually around?" There was an awkward pause and the doctor was quick to explain himself. "I'm not saying this with any sort of intent—it's more just to give you a heads-up as a couple. When Gene comes out of this, there's no telling who he's going to need, who he's going to turn to. It's good if he has a strong, healthy connection with his family."

***

The Barfields fell silent, and Adam in particular felt as though he was caught in a most unwelcome spotlight.

"He has a strong connection," Maren finally said, squeezing little Sophie to her chest.

Adam forced himself to nod in what he hoped to be a casual way.

Gene did have strong connections…just not with him.

The doctors finished the consult and made their leave, and Kendra took an exhausted Sophie home. Maren and Adam stayed where they were, watching the untouched coffee grow cold.

Adam was making a mental checklist. The first thing he was going to do when he got home was bury the dogs. Then he was going to go to the Hess's house and bury their dogs as well. After that, he wasn't sure.

"Call the dean, ask him to find you a substitute for the next few weeks."

Adam glanced at Maren in surprise, but one look at her face told him not to argue.

"We're both going to be here," she continued in a hard, flat voice. "We're both going to be here every second."

Adam nodded meekly. "Yes, of course we will."

Despite his compliance, Maren shot him a hard look from the corner of her eye.

"I told the doctor he had a connection."

Adam's heart skipped a beat before continuing on at double speeds.

"And he does. I promise, Maren. He will."

Chapter 15

When Gene awoke from his procedure, he claimed not to remember what had happened, but the first thing he did was ask as to the condition of his beloved dogs. Both parents clammed up and Gene said nothing as silent tears trickled down his neck and stung his lacerations.

The hospital was more crowded than usual, and he was temporarily sharing a room with a little boy who had broken his leg in a car accident. Their eyes met as Gene was wheeled into the room, but both boys remained quiet, shy of the stranger and the stranger situation. It wasn't until Adam and Maren went to speak to the hospital coordinator to demand some privacy that the boys were finally left alone.

"I'm Ricky," the boy announced unexpectedly, breaking the overbearing silence.

Gene twisted his head as far as he could to see him. "I'm Gene. What happened to your leg?"

The boy looked mournfully down at his neon cast. "My cousin took me out for a ride in his new car. Usually he's really fun, but he was acting weird, and his breath smelled all funny, and we crashed into a pole."

Gene didn't know what to make of this. "Maybe he was sick?"

Ricky shrugged. "Maybe. What happened to you? It looks like you got eaten by a bear."

"Two pit bulls. They jumped over the fence into my back yard." Gene's young face clouded over for a moment as the images flashed before his eyes. "I think my dogs are dead," he mumbled. "No one will tell me anything."

Ricky looked at him sympathetically before glancing again at his own cast. "Yeah, no one will tell me anything either."

"I guess grownups are like that."

"Not all of them." The boy brightened. "Some of them are really great. There's a woman who comes to see me here. I think she works at a church, but she's really cool and she doesn't treat me like I'm a kid."

In unison, both boys rolled their eyes at this universal injustice.

"But why does she come to see you? Do you think she'll come to see me?"

Ricky picked at a stray piece of gauze. "I don't know, probably. Her name's Reverend Carrie. If you ask your nurse about her, I'm sure they'll let her know."

"…finally get through to the man. Honestly, you'd think we were asking an audience with the Dali Lama…"

Gene heard the angry sound of his parents' voices filtering up the hall and he quickly rolled over and pretended to be asleep. At the last moment, he remembered his new friend and waved to say goodbye. Ricky flashed him a smile, and in the age old spirit of comradery, loudly announced to both Adam and Maren that Gene had fallen asleep.

The next morning, in his brand new private room, Gene did in fact ask the nurses about this Reverend Carrie, and she came to visit him the very next day. Adam and Maren were quick to protest this, but at Alta Bates, they believed that medical chaplains were an important part of patient recovery. Their psychologist assured them that he would begin regular sessions with Gene as soon as he was released, and added that if Gene was looking to turn to some higher power to help him deal with his grief, it might be in his best interest if they let him.

So every day, for the full month that Gene was in the hospital recovering from his skin grafts, Adam and Maren stepped out for coffee from precisely eleven to eleven twenty-five to give Gene and the chaplain time to talk.

"How are we doing today, Gene? Feeling any better?"

It had been about two weeks now, and any awkward barrier that might have separated them had long passed. They'd started slowly, first addressing the obvious guilt and loss over Gene's heroic dogs, and had gradually moved on to some of the overriding issues of life and death, as well as the church's prescribed morality, and the daily relevance of God.

"They're taking off the last of the dressings today, so I'm finally going to be able to see my wrists," Gene answered excitedly.

He was thrilled to have discovered a bright light whilst recovering from such a dismal situation, but for a boy of Gene's age and energy, each day confined to a hospital bed was torture.

"That's wonderful! You must be so excited!" She beamed at him. "Plus, I bet it itches."

Gene laughed. "Like you wouldn't believe! So hey — they say I'm probably going to get to go home next week to start physical therapy and get back to school. Were you able to find a church near my house?"

"Not only that, Gene, but I also found a family that lives near yours who said that they can pick you up and drop you off every Sunday."

That was a huge relief. While Gene had latched on strongly to his newfound faith and wanted to pursue his interest in the church, his parents had been less enthusiastic. Although Maren had been raised Catholic, she had discarded all fragments of the religion when she went to college. Adam was a far more predictable story; science was his god. So Gene was left alone, which, ironically enough, was part of the fundamental problem that had driven him to the church to begin with. It filled a deep void somewhere inside that he hadn't ever realized was there.

He'd never felt as though he fit in, or particularly belonged. There was no tangible basis for this, of course…it was more like an existential isolation he'd felt on various levels as long as he could remember. But with the active pre-teen ministry that Reverend Carrie told him about, he was hopeful that he could find some larger purpose to help determine his place in the world.

There was a knock on the door and Adam and Maren breezed into the room, five minutes early.

"All finished?" Maren asked briskly, resenting the constant intrusion from this strange woman.

Reverend Carrie squeezed Gene's foot in goodbye before getting graciously to her feet. "Yep, I was just leaving."

"Go with God," Adam mumbled.

She paused by the door. "I'm sorry Dr. Barfield, I didn't catch—"

"I said go."

She swept out the door without another word and Gene stifled a sigh. They had been growing openly more hostile to her with each progressive visit, and it was getting to the point where he was embarrassed in advance the second he heard them coming up the hall. It was a good thing he was leaving soon. He firmly believed that, given the right circumstances, his father could test even God's patience.

Seven days later Gene was finally released, and the family breathed a sigh of relief as they took him home. No one said a word as he walked past the empty yard with the two soft little mounds against the far fence, and no one said a word as the first thing he did upon entering the house was head straight into his sister's room to hug Sophie.

The very next day a man showed up at the house to begin Gene's physical therapy. Although the plastic surgeon had been one of the best in the business and Gene didn't have any lingering disfigurement or scars, he had still lost muscle tissue in his legs and arms, and required constant, specific exercise to bring him back up to strength.

Adam was thrilled by these sessions. There was finally someone there studying Gene's every move with as much intensity as he. He would sit in on each appointment under the pretext of moral support, and eagerly share notes on development.

At the end of one session, the therapist declared that he had never seen a more attentive parent, a quotation that Adam proudly relayed to Maren at dinner. On the far side of the table, Maren bit back her sarcastic response, but he could read it on her face. *Oh, yeah, you have been attentive in all ways, at all times.*

Observing Gene had never been the problem.

"Where is he tonight anyway?" Adam asked, glancing at Gene's empty chair.

"Church group," Maren replied shortly.

Adam glanced at little Sophie before censoring himself as well. Gene's ongoing obsession with the church was a continued source of annoyance and borderline frustration for both him and Maren. Perhaps if he was content to simply take what he was learning and apply it to his own life, they would be more accepting of it. But Gene was in the early-teen age bracket where they were constantly encouraged to take the church's message outside the walls of the sanctuary, and bring all the ones they loved "into the fold."

***

For Maren, it felt like a religious sentence of parental inadequacy had been laid upon her, and she coldly halted Gene's every effort to reach out and connect. Maren suffered as she felt a religious sense of inadequacy, and coldly halted Gene's effort to reach out and connect. She found the courage to tell Adam that she felt that she had failed, both as a mother and as a wife. As for Adam, he viewed these existential ventures from a purely anthropological standpoint and barely noticed Gene's attempts to get his father to join him. Likewise, he was completely oblivious to how his apathetic refusal devastated the child.

"Put yourself in his shoes," Schulze advised him during one visit. "The boy lost the very feeling of safety in his own home. We both know that you and he don't have the strongest relationship, which only leaves Maren and Lilly — two women he's seeing on an increasingly infrequent basis. It makes perfect sense that he would reach out and try to find something more."

"Yes, but...*God?*" Adam scoffed, unable to keep the obvious displeasure from his face.

"Yes, God, Adam." Her eyes twinkled. "But don't worry, I don't think for a moment that Gene expects the two of you to see eye to eye."

Adam pocketed this slight for later consideration, and mulled over his session as he drove the twelve blocks home. If there was something missing in Gene's life, if he felt adrift and isolated, it would certainly make sense. He was living in a different era than his birthright. He was displaced in both time and history. Adam parked in the driveway and sat there in the dark, trying to come up with a solution. There had to be something he could do to fix these profound, cosmic issues. And then the idea came to him as clear as a bell.

"Maren," he shook her gently awake as he slid into bed beside her, "I think it's time we got another dog."

"Are you serious?" Gene asked as the parents made the announcement over breakfast the next morning. Adam and Maren couldn't tell if he was pleased or not, but little Sophie started bouncing in her chair.

"Yes, yes, can we?!"

"If it's what you two want...," Maren began cautiously, still trying to gauge Gene's reaction. "I thought we could get one for each of you."

Gene seemed to consider this for a long moment before his eyes settled on Sophie's pleading face.

"As long as they're...different," he agreed. "Different kinds than before."

Maren squeezed his hand and Adam nodded vigorously. "That's a good idea. These aren't replacement dogs; they're new dogs. Best to start with a clean slate."

And he wouldn't have to look at that insufferable cotton ball anymore.

After they were finished cleaning up their meal, they piled into the car and drove to the nearest pet store. In many ways it seemed like a sudden change of events, but they still had all the supplies they'd need from the last dogs, and Adam and Maren were secretly hoping that by returning Gene's life to the way it was, he might give up on the whole Jesus-kick.

The kids wasted no time zeroing in on their choices — two golden retrievers. They were sisters, puppies born into a litter of five, and for a daring moment, Gene and Sophie tried to press their luck and see if maybe they could take home the whole litter. One look at Maren's face stopped that venture, and they turned instead to their puppies of choice. Sophie went for the biggest puppy of the group, while Gene selected the smallest. Ginger and Amber. Once more, both children seemed to have the names already picked out by the time they saw the dogs.

As it turned out, "puppy-therapy" was hands down the most effective for Gene. He absolutely delighted in the cuddly little dogs, and took great pride and accompanying them to the puppy classes that were held twice a week at a nearby park. The pit bulls next door had been put down, and after paying an extravagant out of court settlement to the Barfields, the Hesses had moved away. Slowly, the little family was piecing itself back together.

But Maren and Adam were both over-achievers, and the healing wasn't done yet.

"Disneyland!"

Sophie squealed at a frequency usually reserved for canines and opera stars, and Adam ground his teeth together as he tried to find parking amongst the swarms of over-excited families.

This was the last thing, he kept telling himself. The last thing for Gene before Maren's ultimatum was up and he was allowed to return to his work. The thought steadied him as he parked the car and held the kids down as Maren lathered them with sunscreen.

"Now remember," she warned, "we hold hands. There's no running off, and if you...."

"MICKEY!"

And they were off, streaking towards the costumed mouse as he stopped to take pictures and sign autographs for eager children.

Adam sighed. "This is going to be a long trip."

"They're going to love it." Maren squeezed his hand. "Maybe you will too."

But for once, Adam had it right, and the elder Barfields found themselves to be no match for the unending energy of the kids. To her credit, Maren remained at least outwardly calm, but Adam trailed along behind the three of them like a man in a nightmare.

They had to go on every ride—twice. They had to see every cartoon. They made a game of finding the hidden Mickey heads at every attraction. Adam made a game of finding himself more coffee. By the time they took a break for lunch, he felt as though they may well have been at the park for the last thirty years.

"Where am I?" he joked with Maren, staring helplessly around. "Is this real?"

She smacked his arm playfully, but Adam could see the tired bruises already forming beneath her eyes.

"Mommy—can we go to see the princesses after lunch?"

Sophie had been unable to eat, she was too wound up. Her eyes flashed around a hundred places at once, and had settled, hungrily, on the pink castle looming up in the distance.

"Ew, no," Gene complained. "Let's go on the Matterhorn again!"

147

Adam had found this ride unsettlingly ironic and was quick to put the kibosh on that idea. "Tell you what," he compromised. "How about the girls do their princess thing, and you can ride the carousel until they're finished? Then maybe we can all go on Indiana Jones."

Maren glanced up gratefully, surprised by his sudden parental input. "That sounds perfect. We'll meet you at there in about thirty minutes."

They split off their separate ways and Adam took a seat beside another father on a park bench as Gene climbed aboard the massive carousel and selected his steed. It harkened back to his days with Lilly at the zoo, and his face lit up as the music started and they began to spin.

Adam further pondered Gene's psychological make-up as he watched him cheering amidst the other children. It was very difficult to find any characteristics that set him apart from his contemporaries; any overriding difference that would account for his feeling alone and out of place.

He was kind, loving, intelligent, and socially adept. A boy who loved sports, and enjoyed reading and school. Furthermore, he had strong attachments to Maren, Sophie, the pets, and even—more guardedly—to Adam. Considering that this father was so often either absent or conning his way into a blood sample, this was an impressive feat in itself.

Then there was the physical. Nowhere on Gene's face or body would you suspect his extraordinary lineage, and yet, if you knew what to look for, certain attributes were there. His eyes were blue, like Otzi's, and he had a slightly more pronounced brow ridge than was to be expected in a ten-year-old. His teeth had the same separation between the front maxillary incisors as did his biological father's, and likewise, the orthodontist had told Adam that Gene would not be getting his wisdom teeth. None had ever developed.

But he had all of his ribs, whereas Otzi had been missing his twelfth pair, and far from anyone thinking he resembled a Neolithic man, Gene was already a big hit with the girls at school. Adam was therefore left to conclude, he was quite simply, unique. A bridge between two worlds, rather than firmly belonging in either one.

This, he supposed, was the root of Gene's subconscious angst.

"Which kid is yours?"

Adam glanced over at the father sitting beside him gazing at the carousel.

"I'm sorry?" he asked.

The man pointed to a little girl with bright red hair and the telltale, rabid, Disneyland eyes.

"That's my daughter, Olivia. It's her first time here." He chuckled as she clung in delighted terror to her spinning horse. "Which one's yours?"

After a few seconds, Gene came sailing into view and Adam pointed. "That one there."

The man nodded with a smile. "Aw yeah, I can see it."

Bemused, Adam glanced at the man in surprise, before smiling to himself.

Could he now?

Chapter 16

For the next two years each of the Barfields continued on with their separate lives, a family in name but growing further and further apart.

Adam's work with his vaccine had jumped to even higher planes. He'd been flown to five different countries to give speeches on his mounting statistics and results, and rumor had it he was now on the short list to win the Nobel. Maren had continued to teach at the university off and on, but as she was now a key component in running Adam's lab while he was away, there had been a marked shift in her priorities. Meanwhile, Sophie was a very precocious six going on seven, rambunctious, with a burning desire to be the constant center of attention. And Gene?

Gene was spending most of his time at church.

He had enrolled in a confirmations class that ran concurrently with the school year. Every Tuesday he studied at the church for three hours, and for the rest of his week he was usually engaged with some ministry activity or outing with the class. At the end of the two years, he would be baptized and confirmed.

Adam and Maren had persisted in their attempts to dissuade him, but as he neared the end of his study, they began to give up the ghost. He had been incredibly dedicated over the last months, only missing three classes in two years, and it was obvious that he felt the weight of his calling in his very soul. He had also attached very strongly to the church's youth leader, Pastor Glenn.

Glenn was the epitome of everything Gene had been missing in his life. She was thoughtful and attentive. Morally sound and secure. But most importantly, she genuinely cared what was going on inside Gene's head. She became his natural idol and confidant, the person with whom he felt closer than anyone else. A stark contrast to his increasingly absent father.

In what seemed like no time at all to Gene, and an endless purgatory to his parents, the date of his baptism and confirmation was right around the corner. The only thing he needed now was his birth certificate to validate the proceedings. And that would require a talk with his father.

As usual, Adam was deeply involved in his study, and Gene tapped lightly on the door. A moment later it opened and a slightly frazzled Adam appeared in the frame, casually blocking the contents of his desk from Gene's line of sight.

Gene took a step back and momentarily examined his father. His hair had begun to gray, and there was a pronounced thinning in the back. He seemed to have lost weight in some places and gained it in others, giving him the pronounced look of someone who sat in a chair all day. But perhaps the most telling thing was his eyes. They were wild eyes—crazy. As if something was boiling right below the surface, and at any moment it could explode.

"Hey Dad, can I talk to you for a minute?" Adam shifted impatiently. "What is it Gene? I'm working."

"Right." Gene got to the point. "Pastor Glenn needs a copy of my birth certificate to get ready for my baptism and confirmation. Do you know where it is? Mom doesn't, and I've never actually seen it myself."

***

Adam's heart froze in his chest. As he'd built his empire of secrecy and deception, there were a few loose ends that had never been resolved. Gene's birth certificate was one of them.

He masked his panic with an annoyed frown. "Does she really need that to confirm you? I mean, surely Christ knows who you are."

Gene bit his lip to control his temper. "It's so I can become an active and validated member of the church, so yes, I need it. I can get it myself—just tell me where it is."

Adam ran his hands maniacally through his hair and stalled for time. "It's probably still in the storage space we used between houses during the move. That's where most of our important papers are. I'll check it out in the morning and see if I can find it."

Gene smiled faintly. "Thanks. And, um...my confirmation is scheduled for a week from Sunday. Do you think there's any way that you could come?"

"Sunday?" Adam was suddenly all business again. "No, probably not. Gene, you know I usually spend Sunday at the lab." He tapped his fingers impatiently on the door frame until Gene took the hint and started walked away.

"You spend every day at the lab," he mumbled.

Behind the locked door, Adam poured himself a stiff drink and sank into the leather chair behind his desk. He sipped it steadily down, lost in thought, before pulling a silver key out of his wallet and unlocking a file cabinet drawer. There was Gene's birth certificate, right on top.

Adam studied it as he polished off his first drink and started on another. The paper listed him as Gene's only parent. What was the kid going to think when there was no legal mother? Adam and Maren had never even hinted to Gene that his parentage might be anything other than what he'd suspect. He believed Maren to be his biological mother, and had no inkling of his birth, let alone his extraordinary heritage.

In what was becoming a regular nighttime occurrence, Adam's lungs tightened and he felt the overbearing weight of his lies closing in on him.

What was he going to tell him? That he was adopted? It would probably be the easiest solution, but since Adam was listed on the certificate, that wouldn't hold up either. Could he just make a fake one to show the minister? How would the church be able to tell the difference?

He closed his eyes and downed the rest of his bourbon. No, that wouldn't work. Eventually, there was going to come a time when Gene would need to present the paper to a legal authority, and when that time came, the jig would be up. Better to just deal with it now.

But he pictured the devastated look on Gene's face when he told him, and slowly slid the certificate back into the drawer.

Or…he could always deal with it tomorrow.

After a restless night's sleep, Adam woke up with determination and a plan. He would not be held hostage to this. He would not be put on a timeline. After all, this whole confirmation requirement wasn't his idea. It wasn't his fault. In fact…it was the church's fault.

Adam ignored the mental voice asking what his therapist would think about him blaming Jesus, and threw on his jacket. Yes — this whole thing was the church's idea, so it was their problem. And he was just going to have to have a word with them about that.

"I'm here to see Pastor Glenn, please."

The middle-aged woman blinked up at Adam as he swept through the sanctuary doors and into the first office he saw. The little room was warm and welcoming, with the smell of fresh citrus and a little bowl of candy on the desk.

All the better to brainwash you and blindside you about your parentage, Adam thought to himself as the woman stood up to get a better look at him.

"I'm Patricia Glenn. And you are?"

Adam took a step back in surprise. This was the woman who'd commandeered his son? She didn't look so threatening. Soft blonde hair cut into an adult bob, and laugh wrinkles around her eyes. This was the woman causing all his problems?

He crossed his arms authoritatively. "I'm Gene Barfield's father."

A warm smile brightened her face. "Oh — Adam, isn't it? It's such a pleasure to meet you. Gene is one of my prize students."

"Yes, well," he took a seat on the visitor's side of the desk, "he tells me that you're requiring a birth certificate in order for him to pass this initiation you people have?"

"The confirmation." She nodded. "Yes, in order to be an active member of the congregation, for our official records, we like to see a birth certificate."

"Well, that's going to be a bit of a problem," Adam began, wondering how to phrase it. "Gene's certificate got lost. I didn't want to tell him — upset him for no reason. An order has already been sent for a replacement, but I'm afraid it won't get here in time for your ceremony."

Pastor Glenn nodded understandingly. "Oh, I see, of course. Well, we'll go through with the confirmation as planned, and sometime in the next month, Gene can bring in the replacement—"

"Why do you need to see it so badly?" Adam asked suspiciously.

Glenn frowned. "I told you—we keep detailed records of the members of our church. This is especially important in Gene's case, as he has no other family in attendance—"

"So that's what this is about?" Adam demanded. "You're using the certificate as a ransom to get me and my wife to see your little Jesus show?"

There was a screech as Glenn pulled back her chair and got to her feet. "Dr. Barfield, I can assure you that's absolutely not the case. This is standard procedure for those seeking baptism. To be honest, I can't remember a time it's ever been problematic before—"

"Gene can't see his birth certificate."

There was a pause. Adam had gotten to his feet as well, and both adults were breathing heavily, leaning towards each other from opposite sides of the desk.

Glenn finally collected herself and took a step back. "Excuse me?"

Adam closed his eyes in defeat. There was no way around it. "Gene can't see his birth certificate, because it only lists me as his biological father. There's no mother on the paper."

"Can I ask why?" The pastor took a seat once more and gestured for Adam to do the same.

After a second's hesitation, he complied. "His mother was a surrogate in India. Gene doesn't know. He believes my current wife is his mother."

"I see. Well, that certainly complicates things." Glenn was quiet for a long time before she finally spoke. "Adam, I think I know why you came here today, and I want to make something clear to you right now. I'm not going to help you perpetuate this lie to your son."

Adam's blood rose to a soft boil. "You're going to do that to him? You're going to blindside him with this information?"

"I don't believe it's anything *I'm* doing to him. I didn't choose to lie to Gene his whole life, Dr. Barfield; that was you."

The walls crept an inch closer and Adam fidgeted in his chair. "But it will devastate him. I never made any plan as to how to tell him…it's never come up."

The pastor looked sternly over her desk. "I'm not passing judgment or blame, but you have to understand that this is *your* responsibility. This confirmation means a lot to Gene; he's worked very hard for it, and in order for it to happen — he needs that certificate."

"And you couldn't make an exception to —"

"I will not use the sanctity of the church to cover your deception. This is on you. But I can say that, as a person concerned for Gene's well-being, I would hope that you tell him the truth."

Adam wandered out of the sanctuary and back to his car with a heavy heart. He'd admit that trying to corrupt a minister had been a bit of a "Hail Mary," but verbal irony aside, he'd actually believed it might work. Gene was going to be home from school by the time Adam got back, and he'd be expecting either a birth certificate or an explanation.

And for the life of him, Adam didn't know which one he would choose.

"Here it is," he handed the folded paper to Gene, "your birth certificate."

Maybe, if the gods chose to smile down on Adam, Gene wouldn't even notice the blip. He'd either miss it entirely or assume that only one parent was required. Their fragile relationship could go on as it always had, and Gene could get baptized as promised, safe in the knowledge that the two people he'd lived with all his life were, in fact, his parents.

"Why isn't Mom's name on here?"

The gods did not choose to smile down on Adam—he'd given them no reason to.

"Because we were not yet married at the time you were born," Adam replied evasively.

Gene frowned at the paper in confusion. "But she was still my mother; shouldn't she be there in writing?"

Adam looked at Gene's face staring up at him in confusion, and with a sharp pang of remorse he felt a little bit of his heart chip away.

Pastor Glenn was right—this was Adam's fault. Gene didn't deserve the pain Adam was about to cause. He didn't deserve to be lied to and spend every day as a walking science experiment. He was a person. An actual, tangible person who could be hurt and wronged.

Somewhere, in the midst of playing God, Adam had forgotten this.

"Actually, Gene, when I decided I wanted to have a child, I wasn't in a long-standing relationship. Maren and I were barely more than friends."

Gene froze, waiting for more, and when Adam said nothing, he tried to piece it together himself.

"So...Mom—I mean Maren—is not my biological mother?"

Adam shook his head and Gene collapsed into a chair, looking like someone had slapped him in the face.

"Was I adopted?"

"No," Adam said forcefully, unable to cause his son any more pain. "I wanted you to be MY child, so I chose to have a surrogate mother carry you."

Gene's face flushed. "Well, who is she? What is her name? Do I know her?" He paused a second before looking up in shock. "Is it Lilly?"

"No, it's no one you know." Adam pulled up a chair and sat beside him. "She was a woman a clinic hired in India; we never met."

Neither of them spoke for a long time as Adam stared at Gene and Gene stared off blankly into the distance, hands clenched up into trembling fists.

Finally, Adam squeezed his shoulder comfortingly. "Gene...are you okay?"

Gene turned to him in a daze, as if he'd only just realized Adam was there. "I have to go."

With that, he rose robotically from the chair and floated down the hall to his room. Adam looked after him for a moment before glancing at the clock and getting to his feet as well.

"I can't wait to see what she thinks about this," he murmured as he picked up his car keys.

***

As his father went off to therapy, Gene paced in circles in his room. He tried to call Pastor Glenn, but her phone went straight to voicemail and he hung up in despair, looking around the four walls of his little sanctuary before falling onto his bed and staring up at the ceiling.

How could they not tell him? *Both* of them? This whole time he had thought—he had just assumed, of course—that the people who called themselves his parents were *actually* his parents.

But he didn't have any real connections here, did he? The perfect Barfield family. He was only half a member. His sister was sweet, but distant, content to live her own life with her own group of friends. His father had never cared for him, and probably never would. And his mother…wasn't really his mother after all.

And who was his mother? How could you even define it?

He had been carried by one woman, breast fed by another, nannied by yet another, and finally, mothered for many years by Maren. But the actual woman who gave him life? She was a complete mystery.

He stewed for a while longer in his newfound isolation, trying to keep it together and working very hard not to cry, when suddenly he jumped to his feet. All his life he'd felt disconnected, strangely removed from his friends and peers. Well, maybe this was the reason why. This wasn't his world. In fact, his real world was half a planet away.

With a surge of fierce conviction, Gene sat down at his computer and began to research India.

***

Across town, things were hardly going any better.

"Do you believe in God?"

"Oh dear." Schulze took off her glasses and rubbed her eyes. "Feeling frisky today, are we, Adam?"

"I'm serious. Do you believe there's a higher force guiding us?"

"I believe in the possibility, sure."

"But you don't know for certain."

Schulze sighed. "Adam, I'm not sure if anyone can know for certain."

"Gene does."

She looked at him questioningly, and Adam stared down at his hands.

"Gene isn't Maren's biological son. I used a surrogate in India. I told him today."

The look of extreme shock was quickly replaced with a mask of professionalism.

"Was there a reason you did it today?"

Adam gave a wry smile. "You could say *God* made me." When she shook her head in confusion, he clarified, "It was just time."

"And how did Gene react?"

The smile faded and Adam's face turned pale. "He couldn't look at me. He just walked away." The clock ticked loudly on the wall behind them as Adam tried to gather his thoughts. "What should I do?" he asked her beseechingly. "How do I begin to fix this?"

"Adam, at this point, what you do is very simple." She surveyed him over the tops of her glasses and rolled up her sleeves. "You give him whatever he needs."

Adam opened the front door quietly. He had driven around a while after his session and he didn't want to disturb the house if it was asleep. He hung up his jacket on the coat rack beside the door, and when he turned around, Maren was standing behind him in a rage.

There was a sharp crack as she slapped him across the face. His eyes watered automatically with pain, and he held his cheek as they stared at each other in charged silence.

"You told him," she hissed through her teeth. "Without letting me know, you told him."

"Maren—" Adam began, but she spun on her heel and disappeared into their room. A moment later, he heard the door lock.

Casting a weary look at the couch, his new bed for the night, Adam headed slowly down the hall to Gene's bedroom. His talk with Schulze had helped clarify his position, and he was determined to make up for this mess however he could. Whatever Gene needed — it was his.

He had barely touched the door when it flew open and he and his son were standing face to face. He opened his mouth to speak, either to beg or apologize, but before he could say a word, Gene beat him to the punch.

"I want to go to India."

Chapter 17

"What can I say to him, Maren? He wants to go!"

Adam dumped piles of shirts into his waiting suitcase, while Maren hovered around behind him, shadowing his every move.

"You could tell him it's not allowed. You all signed non-disclosure forms for a reason, Adam; this woman does not want to be found."

"We don't know that." He returned to his dresser for pants. "And we owe it to Gene to try."

Maren stepped in front of him in a scarcely controlled rage. "And what if she says no? The clinic hasn't even found her yet and you're already packing your suitcase. What if you fly all the way to India and they can't find her, or she says no?"

Adam sighed. "Then we'll come back."

He moved around her to empty his armload into his luggage and she perched angrily on the bed.

"And what about Gene?"

Adam went for his shoes. "What about Gene? Gene's the whole reason that I'm doing this! Do you think I'd fly all the way to Delhi unless it's what he asked me to do?"

Maren raised her voice. "What about what it will do to Gene if he flies halfway around the world to meet a woman who doesn't want to see him?"

Adam dumped the pairs of shoes into the suitcase and disappeared into the closet before coming up with a handful of ties. "Then at least he'll know he tried."

There was a slight pause and Adam poked his head around to see if Maren had left. He found her sitting like a statue on the bed, pale as a sheet with puffy red eyes.

"Have you stopped for even a minute to consider how this makes me feel?"

When he came up with nothing more than blank confusion, she threw up her hands and wiped angry tears from her face.

"Gene is going off to India to find his *real* mom, and I'll just be sitting here — the lying bitch who pretended to be his mother!"

Adam felt the ties slip from his hands as he watched yet another piece of damage he'd inflicted fall into place. His face fell and he reached out to her.

"Honey, I'm sure he doesn't see it that way —"

"Why am I even asking you? Of course you didn't think of it," she said in disgust, jumping off the bed and heading for the door. "You didn't think to tell me you were ripping our family apart; why would you think about this?"

She didn't come out to the car the next morning to see them off. Instead, she watched from the window, still crying, and looking at Gene as though she was seeing him for the last time.

The ride to the airport was a quiet one, as was most of the flight, even though Adam saw Gene try to mask his excitement as he boarded the big plane for this first ever international flight as a mindful teen. When they landed in Delhi they took a cab to the Nehru InterContinental Hotel, the same place where Adam had stayed so many years before. He'd called ahead to the clinic, and although they were not hopeful regarding the privacy restrictions they'd agreed to meet with the Barfields the very next day. In the meantime, Adam wanted to rest. But Gene, it seemed, wanted to explore.

"I can go out by myself," he insisted, standing impatiently by the door as Adam grabbed his wallet and sat down to put his shoes back on.

"Not in this city you can't. It's too big, and besides, you don't know the language. I don't want you getting lost."

A look of sheer defiance flashed across Gene's face. "Why not? After all, it's kind of my city, isn't it? I'm sure I'd find my way around."

Adam got to his feet and carefully reigned in his frustration. Gene was entitled to his rage. It was perfectly natural that he should feel betrayed and act out. His anger was entirely justified, and Adam was the only person to blame.

"You have every right to be upset, but I'm still your father, and I'm still going to take care of you and make sure you're safe."

Gene scoffed. "Are you my father? I mean, my parentage has been kind of up for grabs lately."

It was a throwaway question, meant only to insult and wound. But its accuracy left Adam badly shaken.

"Come on," he said in a low voice. "I'll show you the temple."

***

A few hours later, Gene was finally tired and Adam was ready for death. They climbed into bed relatively early and slept a solid nine hours before waking up to see the clinic. Gene bounced with nervous energy all the way there, shaken as he anticipated this meeting. He'd known about his actual mother for a total of thirty-six hours, and already he'd crossed the planet to try to find her. She, on the other hand, had known about him since before he was born, and had never made any effort to connect. Maybe what Maren had been yelling about at the house was right. Would she be glad to see him, or would she try to hide him in shame? Since she had known about him since his conception she could not really care...or could she? And as they got close enough to see it, his very heart seemed to tremble in fear.

***

The clinic was exactly how Adam remembered, but the staff had changed. They waited for about twenty minutes in the lobby, Gene tapping his foot nervously against his chair, until the clinic supervisor took them to through the twisting maze of exam rooms back to his office.

"Sorry for the wait, Dr. Barfield," he apologized, gesturing to the two chairs sitting crookedly in front of his desk. "As you can see, we're at peak capacity."

"It's no problem. Gene here just had a few questions we were hoping you could answer."

Gene leaned eagerly forward in his chair. "Yes. Well, I was wondering if you were able to contact my birth mother to see if she would meet with me. I know she signed the privacy agreement, but I thought that maybe if she knew I was here—"

"Yes, she did sign the privacy agreement," the supervisor interrupted him, "and I'm afraid her answer was no." Gene barely had a chance to register this heartbreaking news before the man continued. "We were, however, able to contact your biological mother, and she said she would be very pleased to meet with you."

Gene froze in his chair and Adam caught his breath. Another lie revealed. He didn't know why he hadn't seen this one coming. Of course the clinic would stress this distinction.

"I'm sorry." Gene shook his head, trying to understand. "My biological mother?"

"The egg donor," the man clarified. "As opposed to the surrogate herself."

Adam glanced at Gene apprehensively, but the boy kept his eyes firmly forward.

"Yes. I would very much like to meet with her."

***

It took most of the following morning to rent a car and drive to the Haryana state in Northern India. Adam had tried to broach the subject of the egg donor versus surrogate with Gene last night, but Gene had firmly shut him down. "I should have expected it," was all he'd say.

The further away from Delhi they drove, the poorer the countryside seemed to become. Gene stared out the window as they passed shack after shack, each more decrepit than the last. Little kids, wearing little more than rags, played with toys made out of wood in the mud beside their houses. Elderly people with gnarled hands begged for food and water. And everywhere they looked, there were flies. Flies stuck to people, flies stuck to houses. Flies stuck to everything.

But when they finally arrived at the village in Haryana, a beautiful woman ran out to the car to meet them. She had flowing black hair and high set cheek bones that looked incredibly familiar. Adam turned to Gene in the passenger seat beside him, but Gene had frozen in place, staring with wide eyes out the window.

Adam couldn't help but smile. "Come on. You said you wanted to meet her."

The second they stepped from the car, they were pulled into a warm embrace. The woman may have been slight in stature, but her slender arms gripped them with surprising strength. After a moment she pulled away from Adam, but kept her hands on the sides of Gene's face.

"Gene?" she asked. All he could do was nod and she gave him a blinding smile. "I'm Nandita."

They were shown inside to a cozy little home, small but neat, with the faint aroma of incense and curry. Adam and Gene sat in deeply cushioned velvet chairs, admiring the Indian-style wall murals, while Nandita brought them tea and little cakes, each topped with a single almond.

"So," she said before either of them could speak. "I suppose you want to know why I did it."

Gene's cheeks flushed a dark crimson, but he stared intently into her eyes. "I just don't understand. Was there a reason you did? Why didn't you ever come looking for me?"

Nandita's sparkling laugh filled the warm little room. "I didn't come to look for you because I knew you were with a family who loved you in a home where you belonged." She gripped his hands tightly. "Now, I came from a poor family, and the thousands of rupees I received for my donation made all the difference in the world, but there was an even greater reason."

Her English was very good and the trance-like way in which she spoke carried Adam and Gene back to a different world in a different time. They could almost see the swirling colors and hear the children laughing in the street as Nandita made her way through the village.

"When I was nine or ten, there was a woman in my village. She hadn't been born here, as most of us had, but she was of our same Jat caste, and so when she married the village carpenter, she left her family behind to start a new life in Haryana. It was a rare match. The marriage between her and the carpenter had been arranged, but they'd actually known each other since they were children. They loved each other. I still remember thinking, when I first saw her, that she looked like the happiest bride.

"But her happiness was not to be. A month or two into their marriage, she and her husband realized that she couldn't have children. They did everything they could think of; she took the herbs and remedies prescribed by the local medicine-men, and even went into the bigger cities to speak to the university doctors there. Nothing helped. The woman was disgraced. Where I come from, the greatest thing a woman can do is bring a life into this world. She felt as though her entire purpose was for not. A week later, the happy bride jumped off a bridge into the river and killed herself."

The shocking story ended as suddenly as it had begun, and it left Adam and Gene reeling in the aftermath. But Nandita took a sip of her tea and continued as if nothing had happened.

"It taught me a valuable lesson; never take for granted that with which I had been blessed. A couple of months later I saw a local advertisement; *If you want to serve a noble cause and help an infertile couple find true happiness, please contact us.* It was as if I had been meant to see it. I called the clinic the very next day, and I've been happy about my decision ever since."

Of all the things for Gene to have heard, of all the reasons for her to have given, this was beautiful. She felt called. Gene could certainly relate to that. And because she did so, he was given the opportunity to have a life beyond the staggering poverty he had seen.

He'd read in an article on the flight over that in Indian society, boys remained permanently in their parents' home to take care of them in their old age. When they married, their wives would move in with them as well. For this reason, it was the goal of every couple to have a son, not a daughter. The rate of female infanticide had skyrocketed, as parents who had girls would try again for the desired gender.

What if he had been born here? He wouldn't have the possibility of a university education; he'd be forced to work a labor-based job until he was old enough to die badly in a small house. And what if he had been born a girl? He thought about Sophie and shuddered.

Perhaps Nandita was right. Perhaps he had ended up right where he belonged.

They talked a little more, mostly regarding Nandita's plans to advocate for women's education in her local village, before the sun started to lower in the sky and Adam announced they had to go.

Nandita and Gene embraced warmly again as they parted ways. She kissed him on both cheeks and made him promise to write her the occasional letter. He fervently agreed, intending to send her small sums of money as well. Then he and Adam got back into the car and returned to their hotel. It seemed like quite the luxury after what they'd just seen. After taking long showers to rinse away the exhausting emotional drain, they readied their suitcases and went to sleep early to be ready for their morning flight. They had done what they came here to do.

The flight back to San Francisco was almost as quiet as the one to India, but it lacked the underlying tension. The drive into rural India and the visit with Nandita had opened Gene's eyes. There was a profound beauty to the colors and customs of his biological mother's home, but in no way did he want to be a part of it. Quite the contrary, he shuddered to imagine what his life might have become, and looked forward instead to arriving safe at home in Berkeley.

When they finally pulled up to the house, the first thing Gene did was run inside and grab Maren in a huge hug. Her eyes widened in surprise, but then snapped shut in utter relief as she wrapped her arms around him and buried her face in his hair. Her son had come home to her.

Gene spent the rest of the night alone in his room, obsessively researching Indian philosophy. He was especially taken with the Hindu concept of dharma—the right way of living. As his mind wandered back down the poor yet colorful streets of India, he couldn't let go of the idea that he owed a "life debt." Thanks to Nandita's generosity and open-heart, he had the chance to do just about anything he wanted with his life. And, although it pained him to admit it, this was thanks, in part, to Adam as well.

***

As Gene was toiling away in his room, rethinking his life in a way to accommodate for multiple philosophies, Adam picked up the phone and sat down at the kitchen table. As he started to dial, Maren took a seat beside him.

"Who are you calling?"

"Lilly," he answered, as he punched in the numbers. "Just to let her know that we're back."

Without a word, Maren silently walked to the base of the phone and put her fingers down on the receiver. Adam met her gaze as the line went dead. They stared at each other for a moment in silence before Maren got up and headed to their bedroom. The door closed but didn't lock, and Adam was quick to follow. But when he opened the door, he froze in surprise.

Maren was standing right in the middle of the room.

Naked.

Adam closed the door quickly behind him. Nervous energy coursed through his veins, and he found that his hands were shaking as she walked forward and wound her fingers through his.

"You already know what I'm going to say, Adam, so I'm not even going to say it. I won't share you. I'll never share you again."

He bowed his head, but she lifted it so he was looking into her eyes.

"I just got my family back. We have wonderful little Sophie, and I just got back my son. I need a husband now, not an absent-minded professor. I need someone I can trust."

Adam's lips parted, and he trembled a little in the heat from her body.

"Is that going to be you, Adam?"

And just as Gene was lost in another world, so Adam thought back to all the moments he and Maren had shared. They'd experienced the highest successes and the lowest tragedies. They'd faced their own mortality in Mexico. They'd created one life and raised another. And she had, through all of it, the thick and the thin, been his best and most loyal friend. He loved her.

There was a rare tenderness as he looked down at her face with a soft smile.

"I'm your man."

Chapter 18

Adam was attempting to put his life in perspective.

A brief email was open on his computer screen…a letter requesting a new batch of vaccine with a promise of compensatory funds. Sent to him by the president of the United States.

"Adam, honey, what are you doing in there?"

He closed the laptop in one fluid movement and sat back in his chair, staring at where the email had been.

"Oh, nothing. Just catching up on some correspondence."

"Well, dinner's in five minutes. I made that ravioli dish before the tomatoes could go bad."

He nodded robotically, still staring at the imaginary screen. "I'll be right there."

As fate would have it, the president was not the only one who'd written to him that day. A similar letter had arrived by courier that morning, handwritten by the director of the World Health Organization.

After painting a rather poetic picture of the impact his work was having on the entire global community, it also ended with the promise of payment. When Adam saw the sum they offered, he had to walk three times around his office before settling back in his chair to look at it again.

His plan had succeeded. His dream was complete.

So why did he keep thinking about Otzi?

He'd been up half the night researching the man, studying his lifestyle and habits, wondering how his childhood must have been. He'd been born into a herding society, and had likely begun work as a shepherd at a very young age. His bones showed that he spent his life travelling over hilly terrain, probably with an accompanying dog to help him tend to the sheep.

As Adam's mind wandered, he found it was easy to imagine Gene with his beloved Amber and Ginger, watching over their flock as they sat beneath the expansive night sky. He would probably have taken to it as naturally as he was taking to his life in this century. If there was one thing Adam's anthropological study had shown, it was that human life was very adaptable. It fit in where it found itself.

But the thing that Adam kept circling back to was that when Otzi met his death, he was completely alone. There was no dog or flock. No wife or companion. Just the sound of his own breathing and the overwhelming silence as he slipped away into nothing.

And though he was far from seeking death, Adam felt a strange kinship. Sometimes he felt like all he was searching for was silence. The one moment of absolute quiet. Of peace.

"Adam—dinner!" Maren called impatiently. "And there's a messenger here to see you; says he has some contracts for you to look over?"

Adam roused himself from his reverie and joined Maren at the door. He had every intention of signing both of those contracts, and in order to do so, it was necessary to get Gene to donate more blood so a new supply of B lymphocytes could be cultivated and cloned. The fate of the world rested on the shoulders of a sixteen-year-old boy, and Adam was the only one who knew it.

Thank god Gene was a responsible kid with a good head on his shoulders, or there was no telling what might go wrong....

***

"It's ecstasy," Giselle promised.

Gene took the tiny capsule in his hand and studied it closely. "Are you sure?"

Her dark curls bobbed up and down as she nodded. "My brother gave it to me. He said it was a late birthday present for you, and that we should 'have some actual fun for once.'"

They laughed softly as they considered the pills.

Hard drugs and alcohol were not Gene's usual scene. Quite the contrary, over the last summer he'd grown into the a-typical California boy; tall, handsome, happy, and healthy, raised on plenty of sunshine and good food. His girlfriend, Giselle, was both a cheerleader and a star chemistry student at school. She was a little pixie; a beautiful future doctor who was madly in love with Gene. They'd started as study-buddies, and things had quickly progressed from there. It was impossible to deny the attraction between them, and before long, they were holding hands in the school halls and attending each other's church groups.

But things were progressing in other ways as well. High school was historically a time when the innocent young teens of the world gathered together and lost themselves in a wash of hormones. Gene and Giselle were no exception. What started as a chaste connection quickly accelerated to silent moaning and gropes in deserted classrooms after school. Before long they were taking the time-honored trip to

Planned Parenthood, and making the standard vows for everlasting love.

***

Adam didn't approve. Although he was unaware of most of the ways Gene had strayed from what Adam would define as "an anthropologically sound lifestyle," he had seen the deep attachment building between him and his girlfriend, and had spent many hours fretting as to how this might upset his plans. The entire legacy Adam had been building was predicated on the fact that he could control Gene. He didn't want him making deep emotional connections that might take him away. Not to mention the fact that Adam had intended his ongoing study on Gene to include eventual offspring. For the good of the science, he could only be allowed to procreate with the best. Who knew what kind of genes this girl might have hidden in her family tree? But as much as Adam may frequently forget, he was, in fact, dealing with an intelligent, intuitive boy, not a test monkey.

***

Adam's desire for overriding control was not lost on Gene, any more than his pathetically transparent attempts to come between Gene and the ones he loved. In his reading for sophomore English, he found disturbing parallels between his life and certain themes in *Death of a Salesman*, and it wasn't long before he found himself in open rebellion, threatening to strike off on his own. But every time he would get close to leaving, Adam would sense it and back away, offering some freedom or reward to ease the situation.

This was how Gene acquired the Jeep he and Giselle were sitting in as they contemplated trying ecstasy for the first time.

It was the day after Gene's sixteenth birthday, and he'd gotten permission for an extended curfew from his parents to take Giselle out in the new car for a night on the town. Adam and Maren might have rethought this leniency if they'd realized what he was about to do.

"I think it's just supposed to make you really happy," Giselle mused as she reached for a water bottle in the back seat. "We can take it on the train on the way to the club. That will give it a chance to wear off before you have to drive us back home from the BART."

The more Gene considered the logic in this plan, the more his mind rebelled against the basic premise. What was he thinking? Hadn't he walked the straight and narrow his whole life? Wasn't he the valedictorian who was off to U.C. Berkeley Summer Session in a few months? Wasn't it still his birthday?

He deserved this. He deserved to take a night to get a little wild.

"Screw it." He tossed it back and swallowed with a mischievous sparkle in his eye. "What's the worst that could happen, right?"

Gene and Giselle didn't make it to the club that night.

They took the train ride as usual, intending to meet their newly expanded circle of friends in the current hotspot, but by the time they walked towards the empty warehouse where the rave was in full swing, the effects of the ecstasy had begun to take hold. Walking became tilted, the walls seemed to grow before their very eyes, and the gyrating people inside were like demons, slaves to the ever-pulsating lights and drums.

They took one look inside and backed quickly away to a bench across the street, thankfully missing any cars that might have done them harm. Every sound was magnified, and every sight transformed into strange and fantastical things; some were beautiful and alluring, others frightening and ugly.

Giselle stared at a fire hydrant with a look of pure terror. "I think I want to go home." She danced her fingers across Gene's neck to get his attention. "I think we should go somewhere safe. This place looks angry."

The "somewhere safe" idea resonated with Gene, and for a moment he looked like a little boy again. "We could go to the zoo," he whispered. The bench beneath him seemed to warm with the very thought.

But Giselle was jumping out of her skin at dust and daisies, and they somehow managed to find their way back to the BART. Back in the familiar security of the train, they began to feel some of the nicer effects. They took turns bouncing up and down, screaming in delight at all the stops and cheering when the train took off again. When an irritable businessman coming home from a late night insisted that they make some sort of effort to control themselves, they clung to each other in fright. It turned out to be a very good thing that the man got off at the next station, because the sudden intensity of touch was proving too much for the hapless teenagers.

At first they couldn't keep their hands off each other; it was fortunate that Giselle was wearing such a complicated dress, or the two of them might have started going at it on the train. But soon they branched out to other things. Gene took comfort in the old train seat and buried his head in the soft, buttery leather, while Giselle was wide-eyed and dumbstruck by the length of her own hair.

If they'd had to stay on the train much longer, they may well have become inadvertent YouTube sensations, but as it stood, they stumbled off and made it to Gene's car with relative anonymity.

"This was a great night," Gene said dreamily, as they gazed at the stars through his open sunroof.

They'd finally consummated their drug-infused passions, and had dozed off and on in the car as most of the effects of the drug wore off. When Gene felt like enough of it had cleared from his system, he took them both back to his house, driving carefully in the very center of the road. He parked beneath a tree on his front yard, and twisted happily in his seat to gaze at his girlfriend.

She'd managed to get her clothes back on, albeit backwards and inside out, and was tracing chemistry equations in the fog on the window in sated contentment. When Gene reached for her hand, she turned to him with a smile and an almost inaudible sigh.

"It really has been…a great night."

There was a sudden knock on the windshield and both of them screamed.

"Gene Adam Barfield, do you want to tell me what the hell you think you're doing?"

Gene's face paled as he stared at Adam through the window, and he discreetly locked the doors.

"It's a dad," he gasped in fright.

Adam was unamused and completely out of his element. When Gene had missed curfew, he had volunteered to stay up and wait for him, and he had done so with increasing panic. When he saw the Jeep coming up the street at five miles per hour he'd thought his problems were over; he saw now that they were just getting started.

"Gene, open the door right now."

Gene obediently complied, and the next second his father was half-lifting him out of the car.

"You're going to wait in my study while I take Giselle home, and then you and I are going to have a talk, young man."

"Dad—*wait!*"

Gene grabbed Adam's arm in panic as he climbed into the car, and Adam turned around to see his son was on the verge of tears.

"What is it?" he asked anxiously.

There was a long silence before it seemed Gene was finally able to speak.

"Driving's really hard," he whispered. "Be careful."

Any other time Adam might have laughed. But tonight he just walked Gene safely inside the house before returning Giselle to her parents. When he returned, Gene was sitting precisely in the study where Adam had left him. He blinked innocently up at Adam as his father tried to decide what to do. He didn't have a huge reservoir of parental experience to fall back on. But just as he was about to attempt a rant, Gene murmured mildly, "I guess it's a good thing I probably won't remember this lecture, huh?"

All at once, Adam didn't see a problem—he saw a golden opportunity.

Keeping his eyes on Gene the entire time, he reached into his wallet and slowly extracted a silver key. Then, with a stern smile meant to put the boy at ease, he crossed the office behind him and silently locked the door.

***

Gene didn't remember anything the next morning. He was unaware of the small mountain of notes Adam had taken by interviewing him in his study. He didn't know his muscles were sore because Adam had been testing his reflexes. He didn't know the bandage on his arm was because his father had taken a small bucket of his blood.

The Band-Aid scared him. He was well aware of the dangers of sharing needles at parties, and although he couldn't recall any such encounter, the evidence was clear. As it turned out, Giselle had walked straight upstairs and fallen sleep on the foot of her parents' bed, so she was pretty much grounded until the end of the school year anyway. And so, frightened and punished, they swore off any future such adventures, and focused instead on their studies.

Both he and Giselle had been accepted for the U.C. Berkeley Summer Session, and even more importantly, Gene had put in an application to spend two semesters studying abroad. It was incredibly unlikely that he would be allowed to go as a junior, but Gene couldn't help but hope.

Now that the initial shock had worn off and he wasn't approaching the country as the prodigal son, he found himself incredibly eager to get back to India. He was fascinated by his people's culture and customs, and was desperate to spend more time with his would-be family.

The plans were set, the books had been purchased and read, and it seemed that all Gene had left to do was wait for the summer session to begin.

Until he got a call from his school counselor.

"How would you like to do your junior semesters in India, and then take the summer session the following year?"

Gene blinked. "Is that even possible? I mean—it was such a long shot—I don't have anything ready, and it's coming up really soon...."

"Logistically, there isn't enough time for you to do both. But when your test scores and writing samples got you entry into the program, the school board thought it was too great an opportunity for you to pass up."

Gene beamed with pride as his mind whirled with the details. When he said he didn't have anything ready, what he meant was, he hadn't told anyone yet. Not his family. Not Giselle.

What would they say about him leaving? Would they be angry? Or maybe even proud?

"I know there are personal things to consider, but the clock's ticking. If you want to make this happen, we're going to need time to coordinate with the school in India. Take a few days and let me know after the weekend."

"I will," Gene promised. "Thank you!"

The first thing he had to do was talk to Giselle. He'd tackle the rest of his family later.

"Hey babe, so I've decided to leave you to fly halfway around the world and spend the next year living in squalor and filth. That's cool, right?"

Gene frowned as he considered his speech. Maybe he should rework the introduction.

Much sooner than he was prepared for, he found himself standing on Giselle's doorstep. Her permanent grounding had restricted her afterschool movements to the confines of her house, so Gene had found himself spending an exorbitant amount of time here the last few weeks. He rang the doorbell and waited until Giselle's father pulled it open with a sarcastic smile.

"Do I know you? You look familiar," he joked. "Perhaps you're the boy who's been haunting our guest room."

Gene grinned. "Hey, Mr. LaRue. Is she home?"

LaRue put on a look of mock consideration. "Where else would she be? Out on the streets taking ecstasy? Or upstairs, in the safe confinement of her room?"

Giselle was lucky in that her family had a rather all-inclusive sense of humor. But it certainly didn't excuse her from serving the full sentence of her punishment.

Gene chuckled nervously, skittering around her imposing father and heading upstairs. "I told you, that wasn't me...that was Giselle's other boyfriend."

After the cursory knock, he slipped inside and found Giselle listening to music on her bed, bored out of her mind.

"Thank God you're here!" she exclaimed, getting to her feet. "I was actually looking forward to doing homework to distract me."

He smiled back at her, but it faded the longer he looked at her face. Finding himself even less prepared for this moment than he'd imagined, he took her by the hands and sat them back down on the bed.

"Actually...I was hoping we could have a little talk."

There were some tears, along with some hard questions, but overall, it wasn't nearly as bad as he thought it would be. Gene replayed the conversation in his head as he headed back to his own house. At first she thought he was only going to get away from Adam, but the more he talked it out and explained, the more she realized he had to go. It seemed as though a huge part of him had always been missing. Now that he knew where to look, maybe he could finally find whatever it was he'd been searching for. In the end, she'd kissed him and given him her blessing, promising to wait for him until he returned.

"Yes, you can go, Gene Barfield, as long as you remember the most important thing." She'd leaned in until their noses were touching with an impish grin.

"What's that?" he'd asked, grinning back at her.

"We still have a date for the prom."

If only his conversation with his family would go as smoothly. He pulled up to his house with a heavy heart and walked slowly inside. Everything bustled around him as usual. Sophie was chatting on the phone to one of her obnoxious friends, Maren was dictating notes to herself on a tape recorder as she set the table for dinner, and his father was nowhere to be seen.

Could he really do this? he wondered as he walked aimlessly through the house. Could he really leave behind everything he knew to live in squalor with a group of strangers?

He knew all the reasons he wanted to go. It was the same existential crisis that had plagued him since childhood. He wanted to find a place where he felt at home. Where he didn't feel slightly out of step with everyone around him. He wanted to belong.

But what would he be leaving behind?

He circled through the house a second time as he tried to take stock, ending up back where he'd started in the living room. It eluded him. But then his eyes came to rest on the locked door of his father's study, and the answer was suddenly clear.

Nothing he would miss.

Chapter 19

India turned out to be hot, and humid, and boisterous, and blossoming….

…and a *huge* mistake.

When it was finally time for Gene to board the plane back to San Francisco after two grueling semesters overseas, he practically jogged down the walkway. At last, he was going home.

From the moment he'd stepped out of the cab at the Gurugram Boarding School, he'd known something was wrong. It didn't remotely resemble the pictures he'd been sent in his welcoming brochure. In those images, it was imposing and huge, rising up out of the Indian jungle like a beacon of light for all who sought to learn. In reality, it was small and rather backwards, a stone's throw away from a convenience store across the street where the students bought cheap cigarettes and beer.

The classrooms were underequipped, and the food and plumbing systems left a lot to be desired, but perhaps the most succinct way Gene could describe his experience in

India was with the age old saying, "boarding school is an education in and of itself."

The boys who had been so friendly and welcoming during his counselor-guided tour were really waiting to discover his vulnerabilities. They viewed the "white boy from California" as an inherent threat, and they made sure to let Gene know that on every occasion they could. Cruel tricks and pranks became a regular way of life, and Gene quickly learned to keep to himself, spending most of his time hiding out in his room or the school library.

Every weekend he went to Haryana to see Nandita, but the visits were becoming borderline depressing. He felt no sense of homecoming or belonging. In fact, he usually left feeling a little queasy from the food and the intense heat. Nandita's husband was an abusive misogynist who strutted around like a game cock, looking for every possible opportunity to cut Gene down to size. Not only did he not seem to realize that Gene, through Adam, was largely financing his little family, but Gene got the distinct impression that if he ever did fully understand this, he probably wouldn't care.

Even the Hindu religion, Gene's last ditch effort at finding his "missing piece," was interesting enough, but did not actively beckon to those not born into it.

Everywhere he went, he felt alienated and alone. He missed his family and their dinners out on the porch. He missed Giselle and Pastor Glenn. He perhaps missed hamburgers most of all. As he was heading back to the dorms one night and crossed paths with a man walking his two dogs, he almost started to cry.

He did make one friend, a smart and outgoing boy named Ash.

They did their homework assignments together, and enjoyed playing tennis and working out in the gym. Ash even invited Gene to his home for spring break so he wouldn't have to stay by himself in the dorms. And while Gene appreciated his hospitality, seeing Ash's happy family, when he knew that his own was halfway around the world celebrating a holiday that didn't exist where he was, only made him even more homesick.

He began striking off the days on his calendar until he could return home, and on the morning of his flight, he bid farewell to Ash and hopped into the cab without looking back. He might have been a wonderful friend in another place and time, but it was not *Gene's* place and *Gene's* time.

He knew where he belonged. And he was headed there right now.

"I'm home!" he called as he pushed open the familiar, childhood door.

There was a thundering from overhead, and then Sophie appeared at the top of the stairs. "Gene! You're back!" She seemed to take flight, jumping the stairs three at a time, until she crash landed in her brother's arms. "I missed you so much!"

He laughed and pulled back to get a good look at her. "My God, Soph, you look so much older."

She beamed smugly. "Maybe that's why I have a boyfriend."

Gene raised his eyebrows and took a step back. "Is that right? Mom and Dad are letting you date at your age?"

"Mom thinks Steven is great, and you know Dad—he doesn't care."

"Steven is a stupid name," Gene mumbled as he tried to calm the protective beast raging in his chest. "Where are Mom and Dad anyway?"

Sophie hesitated a moment before snatching up her cell phone. "Mom's actually at an auction, but she says she'll come home right after; and Dad's still at the lab."

Gene blinked. It had been months, and they weren't even there to greet him?

Sophie sensed his distress and waved the phone in the air between him. "But that's good because I'm here, and now you and I can hang out. Do you want to order a pizza or something?"

He was about to decline and stop by and surprise Giselle instead, but on second thought, he decided to stay. After all, Giselle knew he was coming home today, and he hadn't gotten so much as a text. His eyes fell on Sophie, waiting excitedly for his decision, and his face broke into a huge smile.

"That sounds awesome — you have no idea how much I've been missing American food!"

Five slices and two horrible action flicks later, Sophie was passed out on the couch and Gene was examining a picture of his family as the TV sporadically lit up his face. On the surface, it seemed normal. All four of them were smiling happily at the camera as Sophie and Gene held the two dogs. But Gene remembered the day.

Adam had been two hours late and Maren had to pay the photographer extra to stay and wait. By the time he got there, she wasn't speaking to him. The night before, Sophie had decided to streak her hair green, and they'd just finished getting her washed and dried before they took their poses. Even one of the dogs had been sick — Gene couldn't remember which one. He set the picture down with a sigh and glanced at his snoring sister before staring about the empty house.

There's no place like home.

The next few weeks raced by as junior year was quickly coming to a close. Although he had woken on the couch the next morning to doughnuts and apologies, there had been a decided shift in the atmosphere since he'd left.

Maren seemed to have moved on without him, focused entirely upon her darling Sophie. His father was as distant as ever, asking the same sorts of strange questions he'd been asking all Gene's life, and staring at him like he was under a microscope.

Things had even cooled down with Giselle. Eight months was a long time to test a young relationship, and the distance had definitely taken its toll.

They still had a blast together at the prom. Giselle wore an enchanting strapless gown with an intricate black and white patchwork design, and looked striking next to Gene in his tuxedo. They danced and danced the night away and thoroughly enjoyed the spiked punch, until at last, it was time for the breakfast buffet, and then the monumental event was over.

A week later, Giselle and Gene broke up.

It wasn't exactly a shock for either of them, nor was it the worst thing in the world, and Gene found that it was remarkably easy to turn his attention to bigger and better things. The U.C. Berkeley Summer Session would be starting soon, and he was sure there would be plenty more fish in the sea. There was just one little thing he had to take care of first.

Gene threw down his pencil in triumph with twenty minutes to spare. He doubted he would have even needed the two SAT prep courses Maren insisted he take. Standardized tests were a bit of a joke, and he wondered if anyone else found the essay prompt, "Can people ever be truly original?" as ironic as he did.

And so, with an exceptional score of twenty-one hundred tucked in his back pocket, Gene found himself on Adam's campus for the U.C. Berkeley Summer Session.

Although he had stopped in once or twice to see the absent professor, his father never seemed to have very much to say. In fact, the sight of Gene in the lab seemed to disturb him profoundly, and after two failed attempts, Gene drove straight home after class. He wasn't particularly bothered by this; Adam rarely initiated contact. In fact, Gene had been bowled over the other night when they'd had a sustained conversation after dinner about his research project on Otzi.

As he sat down that afternoon to organize his notes, he secretly hoped to find more compelling details with which to tempt his father into a talk.

The paper was already nearly completed, with only the last few pages missing, and all Gene was looking for today were little embellishments to fill it out. He sighed and took a swig of water as he opened his books and typed in yet another Google search. He was not disappointed. The very latest news flash regarding the DNA sequencing in process for the Y-chromosome in Otzi's group had been identified, and just as it had been in the mtDNA, there were no living descendants. As Gene scribbled this down, he thought of poor old Otzi and his two-inch long penis. No wonder there were no living descendants.

Thank God summer was drawing to a close. As much as Gene enjoyed reading about withered mummies, he was ready for a bit of a vacation before his senior year began. But before he could pack up his bags and head out into the sunlight, he had one last project to complete.

At the very beginning of the Berkeley Session, the students had swabbed the inside of their cheeks in order to extract and classify their own DNA. Once collected, the sample had to undergo numerous tests and procedures before it could be ready for classification. It had been a lengthy process, and one that Gene had greatly enjoyed, but it was almost finished now. Over the next few days, they would finally begin to see the results.

***

And over the next few days, Adam felt as though he was having a heart attack.

Were the fates so cruel that this perverse series of events had come together at precisely the wrong time, for precisely the wrong people? Adam could not believe it to be so.

Not only had Gene come home the other night and announced that the focus of his research paper was — wait for it — Otzi, but he had followed it up with a casual "And we're going to be coding our DNA next week in class." At the same time, a recent controversy over the discovery of the mummy was sweeping the globe, gaining international attention, and a letter to schedule a tentative interview with the people who distributed the Nobel was waiting on his desk.

After all these years, over a decade of careful manipulation and planning, could this be the week that everything came crashing down on his head?

Adam didn't go to work the next day. In his defense, the overwhelming stress and feeling of impending doom had actually made him sick. Instead, he settled on the couch, wrapped in a blanket, and waiting for Gene to come home.

As the hours crawled slowly past, he prayed to a god he had scorned for a way out.

Maybe the sample had gotten contaminated, or Gene had inadvertently screwed up the lab results. One wrong number, one imprecise calculation, and Adam's whole world could be salvaged. He wished he had known what the class was doing earlier; he could have broken into the lab and done a bit of sample contamination himself. In the grand scheme of things, it would have been the least of his crimes.

Crimes? Actual criminal misconduct? When had he become a criminal?

Adam was still asking himself this vital question when the door banged open and Gene stormed inside. Adam was on his feet in an instant. His son was clutching a paper in his hand and looking like the devil himself.

"What is it, Gene? What's wrong?" Adam's voice was little more than a scratch, and he cleared his throat to be understood.

"I can't believe it," Gene was muttering, crumpling the paper in his fist.

Adam tried to clear his throat again, but his mouth was too dry. "Can't believe what?" he croaked.

Gene leveled him with his eyes. "My DNA results came in today, and do you know what they said?" Adam shook his head in silence, and Gene continued to rage. "Mind you, I'm very sure of this. I've been writing about him for weeks, and I just copied his DNA sequence into my paper this morning, so I'm positive I'm right."

"Right about what, Gene?"

The boy finally stopped pacing and threw the results down on the coffee table in between them.

"These DNA results aren't mine." His face grew dark with rage. "They're Otzi's."

Chapter 20

Adam held his breath and waited for the explosion. "Otzi?"

Gene ignored him, pacing around in circles, lost his own world. "I just can't believe it." he muttered in a boiling rage. "*Can't* believe it! After all this time...." He finally looked up at Adam, and his face fell with a defeated sigh. "After all the work I put into this project, someone decides it would be funny to ruin my results by splicing in the sequence from my research project."

Adam exhaled with a bark of laughter and Gene shot him an odd look.

"I'm sorry," he explained with a gasp. "It's just...well, I guess I'm not sure I understand your generation's humor."

Gene rolled his eyes and forced himself to smile. "Anyway, I talked to my teacher about it, and he said that since all my notes and procedure were correct, that I'd still get high marks."

Adam was utterly euphoric; he was having a hard time concentrating on anything Gene had to say. His son's DNA results had come back as Otzi, but somehow, Adam's secret was still safe...they thought it was a joke! His heart slowed back to a normal rhythm and he found himself crossing the living room and giving Gene an unexpected hug.

Gene stiffened in surprise and awkwardly patted his father's back. "Yeah, um, I guess I'm really happy too."

After a moment, Adam grinned, tousled Gene's hair, and pulled away. "Well, kids will be kids. I'm sure whoever did it didn't mean any harm."

Gene shrugged. "It doesn't matter anyway. Professor Shields took a blood sample from me after class, and said he'd rush through the results so I could present them with my finished project."

Adam stiffened as though someone had stuck him with a knife. "Professor Shields?" he asked innocently. "Jim Shields?

"Oh my dear lord...."

***

Professor Jim Shields stared at the printed readout in his hand. It was a Friday afternoon and he had stayed after class to rush through a DNA test for one of his students. Normally he wouldn't do this kind of thing himself, but the kid, Gene, was one of Jim's favorite students, and it appeared he had been the victim of a terrible prank.

More terrible than either of them had begun to realize.

Still studying the paper in his hand, he moved robotically to the coffee maker and started brewing a fresh pot. This was going to take a while.

The sun had slipped low in the sky by the time Jim and the lab equipment called it quits. They had done all they could do. There was no getting around it—it was official.

Otzi was Gene's biological father.

His phone buzzed for the millionth time and he put it on vibrate as he rubbed his eyes and stared again at the numbers. How could this be? How was it physically possible?

His first reaction was an overwhelming wave of pity for Gene. Whatever series of events had transpired to make him what he was, they certainly weren't his fault, and Jim's heart went out to the boy. But whose fault was it? How, in the name of heaven and hell, had a mummy who had been dead for over five thousand years fathered a child in Berkeley?

His phone buzzed again and he looked down with irritation. The number wasn't listed amongst his contacts, but it did belong to the university. With a slight frown and a growing feeling of foreboding, Jim rummaged around in his desk until he came up with his school directory. Going down the list of faculty extensions, his finger came to a sudden and decisive stop.

Adam Barfield.

The famous geneticist. World renowned. Lauded. Too lauded to leave his new Porsche in the faculty parking lot. With people from The Nobel Foundation banging down his door.

If only they knew.

His phone buzzed again, and this time Jim snatched it up with purpose. "Adam...." It took everything he had not to growl. "I thought it might be you."

There was a slight pause on the other end and Jim heard frantic breathing.

"Jim...I was hoping to get a minute of your time. Is it all right if I stop by your office?"

Jim almost laughed out loud. "Hoping to get a minute of your time." This from the man who didn't have time for anyone. He had always been slightly off—peculiar, one might say. But after the overwhelming success of his vaccine, he had become positively unbearable.

"Actually, Adam, I'm in the middle of trying to figure something out. Give me a little time; how about you come by in an hour or so?"

Jim could feel the nervous energy coming through the phone.

"Fine," came the short reply. "That would be fine. I'll see you then."

Exactly sixty minutes later there was a sharp knock on the door. Jim's computer was still warm and humming from his recent investigations, but he sat behind his desk looking steady and calm.

"Come in," he called.

The door opened and Adam rushed through. It took him a minute to orient himself, as he hadn't spent much time recently in this part of campus, before he spotted Jim in the corner and quickly crossed the room.

Jim gave him a faint smile but didn't stand. "Adam, it's good to see you. We don't see much of you around these parts lately."

Adam looked flustered and distressed. His eyes darted frantically around the little room where his calamity had happened, and it took him a second before he gathered himself enough to sit.

"Yes, well, I've been very busy. What with the vaccine and all...."

Jim leaned forward with a wide smile. "Ah yes, the 'Barfield Miracle Vaccine.' I hear you're being considered for the Nobel...is that true?"

"Listen, Jim—"

"I think it's better if I do all the talking, if it's all the same to you."

The conversation froze to a chilling halt as Jim glanced down at a small stack of papers beneath his hand.

"Actually, I've been rather busy myself tonight. You see, the strangest thing happened. We're doing DNA testing in my class this week, teaching the kids how to classify and code, when one of my students came up to me with a dilemma." Jim's face grew protectively grim. "He'd gotten back his results, same as anyone, except his didn't seem possible. In fact, there was only one other person on the planet with his sequence, and he'd been dead a couple of thousand years."

Adam was barely breathing, but Jim was just getting warmed up.

"I was puzzled. At first I thought the student had made a mistake — kids will be kids, you know? But this wasn't the kind of boy to make careless errors. In fact, he's one of the brightest students I've ever had. So I took it upon myself to run his results again after class."

He lifted up the top sheet of paper, and there it was, for all the world to see.

"What do you know? He was right."

A thin layer of sweat appeared on Adam's forehead and he gripped the arms of his chair. "Jim, I can explain."

"Actually, I don't think you have to." Jim's voice had grown very quiet. "I have it all recorded here. I did a little digging after we talked on the phone, and the pieces just fell into place. You were on sabbatical in the Italian Alps the very day Otzi's body was discovered. Nine months later, you come back from India with a mysterious new baby boy. No one asks questions, because, why would they? Who could possibly suspect? A year after that, an immune-enhancing vaccine with the power to stop AIDS and cancer hits the market. Everyone's so thrilled, so busy congratulating you and writing your name on awards, that they don't think it's strange, even for a minute, that you never revealed the name of the donor."

There was hard silence between them as Adam's hope of resolving this quietly was quickly stripped away.

"Did I leave anything out?"

Adam shook his head. He couldn't speak. He didn't know what he'd even say.

"How did you get the sperm?"

A rush of defiance washed over Adam as this lesser mind continued his interrogation. "Well, he refused to ejaculate in my hand," he countered. "It took some knife work, but not much."

Jim was not amused. "Does Gene know?"

The angry façade vanished and Adam hung his head. "No, he doesn't."

Jim took a deep breath, head spinning as he decided what he wanted to do. He had half suspected that Adam was going to deny it. Deny everything in a fiery argument that would rage on for hours. When he looked at the broken man in front of him, he changed his plans.

"I'm not going to go public. I'm not going to do that to Gene. But I will not sit by and watch as you defraud the scientific community to which I've dedicated my entire life. You will withdraw your name from Nobel consideration."

Somewhere, a little light inside Adam died. But he nodded his head in ready compliance.

"And you'll tell Gene."

Adam looked up in panic. "I don't know how. It will…it will break him. I can't do that."

Jim glared across the desk. "You already did break him. Now you need to help him put the pieces back together. And you can start doing that by telling him the truth."

A meeting was scheduled for the three of them the next morning in Jim's office. Both Jim and Adam hoped it would feel like neutral ground. But before he could break the news and come clean with his son, Adam had to talk with Maren.

She just sat and stared. That was all she could do. Long minutes dragged by with Maren frozen on the bed, blinking at Adam like a damaged statue who couldn't quite seem to cry.

"You sick bastard."

Adam bowed his head. "I wanted to do something great...I wanted to help people."

"No, Adam, you wanted to *be* great. And you didn't care how many people you had to break to get there."

"Maren, Gene may not be my biological son, but I've always treated him like—"

"You treated him like a walking petri dish!"

The shriek rang out in the open air, and Adam was glad both Gene and Sophie were out with friends tonight.

Maren got shakily to her feet, but Adam met her head on. He was not the only one who'd been an absent parent.

"Like you even care anymore! Ever since Sophie was born, she's the only child you've been interested to have."

Maren bristled. "Well, someone had to be interested in her! It's not enough that you create one child from a mummified ice corpse, you completely ignore the other!"

"Gene isn't just some *creation*, he's my son—"

"He's not your son, he's your project!" The words seemed to take the rest of the fight out of Maren. She'd been fighting for almost two decades. She was done. "And I can't be here when you tell him." She crossed the room to her dresser and began pulling out clothes. "Sophie and I are going to stay with my sister."

She didn't want to leave Gene alone, but how, at this point, could she help him? What other option would her added presence bring? He could talk to the man who pretended to be his father, or the woman who pretended to be his mother. Either way, it would do no good.

She scribbled a hasty note and left it on Gene's dresser while he was sleeping that night. Ten minutes later, she loaded a drowsy Sophie up in the car and headed south.

Adam couldn't sleep at all, and when the first strains of sunlight rose over the golden Berkeley hills, he was unsurprised to hear a knock on his office door. He opened it to see Gene standing there in his pajamas, looking sleepy and confused as he held up Maren's note.

"What's this all about?" he asked with a yawn. "Mom said that she and Sophie are taking a girls' trip to Aunt Rebecca's, but that she 'loves me forever' and she'll see me soon?"

A probable excuse flew to the tip of Adam's tongue, and he realized, with a great deal of disgust, that it was his automatic impulse now to lie. Instead, he patted Gene lightly on the shoulder.

"Get dressed. We're going out this morning; I need to talk with you."

***

The three of them sat in Jim's office as a heavy silence blanketed the room.

Gene was in absolute and utter shock. His skin was pale and cold, and he looked as though he was going to pass out. Jim tried to catch his eye, to give him some kind of show of support and encouragement, but Gene only had eyes for his father — his *fake* father.

"I think I knew," he finally said, the words coming out as little more than a whisper. "On some level...I think I almost knew."

Adam took one look at the boy's face and *he* knew — his house of cards had finally fallen.

"Gene —"

"How have you been getting my blood?" Gene interrupted, but then his face darkened in understanding. "The night of the party...." His voice trailed away.

Jim gently interceded. "Gene, would you like some water or some air? We can take a break for a minute — give you some time?"

"No, I'm fine," Gene answered with a grim and tearful smile. "I mean, it makes sense; I get it now. Why I always feel like I don't belong...it's because I don't."

Adam's heart broke. "Gene, that's not true —"

Jim held up a hand to stop him and turned to his favorite student. "This is your home. You may have been conceived under extraordinary circumstances, but the universe aligned so that you ended up right here. In this time, in this place. As a scientist, I can tell you, there could be no greater proof that you belong right where you are."

Silent tears trickled down Gene's face as he looked up at his professor.

"Furthermore, your very existence has saved many thousands of lives. You've made a single-handed impact on the world as a force for good. Not many people can say that." He reached out and squeezed Gene's shoulder. "I know you're in a world of hurt right now, but try to keep in mind...there's a silver lining to everything."

Gene's face grew hard and he looked at Adam.

"Yeah, there is. You're not my father."

Jim glanced at Adam, but Adam seemed incapable of speech, staring at Gene like he was seeing him for the very first time. A brilliant boy with a beautiful soul.

…who was lost to him forever.

"So I guess I'm going to be a freak now, huh?" Gene wrapped his arms protectively around his chest as this newfound implication sunk in. "The whole world's going to know that I'm the child of a caveman. I'll never be able to get married, have kids. My life is pretty much over."

"That's not true," Jim hurried to reassure him. "Gene, I'm not going to tell anyone what I found, and your fa — Adam — has been keeping this quiet for years. No one's going to know unless you decide to tell them. Your secret is safe with us."

If only it were true.

Chapter 21

The newspaper arrived the next morning. The lawsuit arrived two hours later.

Son of Famed Geneticist Adam Barfield Descendant of Otzi!

Adam stared down at Gene's eleventh grade photo with ice in his heart. How had this happened?

Avoiding the gawking stares and whispering of his neighbors, Adam snatched up the paper and hurried inside. He'd left a message with Maren, but had received no reply. Gene had refused to come home with him yesterday, choosing to stay over at Pastor Glenn's, and Jim was just as baffled and furious as Adam.

Who'd called the reporter? Who'd spilled the beans?

On a whim, Adam dialed Dr. Schulze's private number. It rang once before it was sent straight to voicemail. Great, he thought, sinking down into a chair in the kitchen. Even his therapist had given up on him.

A short while later, there was a knock on the door.

"Are you Adam Barfield?" asked a young man in a power suit.

Adam looked him up and down in a daze before nodding his head.

"You're being served. Your presence, as well as any and all evidence linking you to the desecration of the mummy Otzi and the subsequent creation of an illicit medical serum, are to appear before Judge Eccles this coming Monday. A failure to appear and produce such evidence will result in increased prosecution and criminal charges."

The man glanced inquisitively at Adam's face before flashing a quick smile.

"Have a nice day!"

The trial. The article. It was all unravelling so fast.

Adam needed to know what had happened. Why now? Who could possibly hate him so much that they'd crucify them before the world, dragging Gene along with him?

There was another knock on the door, and Adam pulled it open with a heavy heart, expecting the young man had more bad news he'd forgotten to tell him. His face clouded and his mouth fell open in surprise when standing on the other side was not a man, but a woman.

"Kendra?"

They sat across from each other at the kitchen table like two sides of an army, each daring the other to advance. Adam felt like he'd been slapped in the brain. He could not believe his ears.

"You did this...," he stumbled, unable to process it. "Why?"

Kendra glared back at him with a steely fire he hadn't known was in her. Without saying a word, she reached into her bag and slammed a large stack of files down on the table.

At once Adam recognized his notes. The years of careful documentation as to every stage of his elaborate plan. Otzi's sperm. Gene's conception. The vaccine. The study. It was all there.

"How did you get this?"

Her eyes narrowed. "Does it really matter? I lived with you off and on for ten years, Adam. It wasn't that hard. I got curious one day after Gene came out of the office with another nasty bruise on his foot. He was always bruised after he played with you. I poked around your office the next day and found this. I couldn't believe it."

Adam's thoughts were a blur. Kendra? Of all the people. And how had she done it?

"My files are locked...," he murmured. "I always keep them locked."

She scoffed. "You forgot to pick Sophie up from school twelve times in the second grade. You think you always remember to lock your files?"

"But why now, Kendra? If you've known for all this time—"

"I kept my mouth shut for *Gene*. For years I kept your dirty little secret because Gene didn't know, and I would never do anything to hurt him. Even when he was at the hospital and they couldn't match his blood, I kept my mouth shut."

"So why—?"

"Imagine my surprise yesterday, when I'm driving home and I see Gene walking along the side of the freeway. I pulled over immediately and ran out to see what was wrong, but he couldn't stop crying long enough to tell me. I drove us to a little coffee shop and he told me the whole story. His father was a monster. A monster who created a freak." Adam winced against the word, and Kendra's eyes shot venom. "You destroyed him, Adam. And I couldn't let you get away with it."

"But look what you've done to him!" Adam rallied in a rage. "You've exposed him, you've ruined his whole life—"

"Gene is strong," came her fierce reply. "He's a walking miracle who's going to go on to save millions of lives. He might hate me now, but someday he'll be glad that he doesn't have to live every minute of his life as a lie. Like his 'father.'"

Just like his "father."

***

It was the trial of the decade. A virtual execution on an international stage.

Adam sat low in his chair as one by one, they came forward to testify against him. Kendra, Markus Pirpamer, the director at the clinic in Delhi. Even Elsie Conway made an appearance.

"Well…it was a long flight and we talked about so many things, but I do remember he made a joke. Something about 'touching a dead man's penis.'"

Adam closed his eyes and sunk even lower in his chair.

Maren and Sophie were not there to witness the spectacle. They'd decided to stay at her sister's house until the worst of the storm blew over. Gene was holed up in the spare room at Pastor Glenn's and refused to take Adam's calls. Even Dr. Schulze had yet to get back to him.

When it was time for the judge to read the sentence, the entire courtroom seemed to hold its breath. Everyone— except Adam. He simply couldn't bring himself to care. Innocent or guilty, what did it matter what a jury decided?

He was guilty. And everyone there, including Adam himself, knew it to be true.

"On the count of willful destruction to an unmarked human burial, the bench finds Adam Barfield guilty as charged."

There was an instant buzz of conversation, but it was silenced with the judge's stern look.

"However, in light of Dr. Barfield's unparalleled medical contributions to an ailing world, the Italian Republic has agreed to wave a prison sentence in lieu of a thirty thousand dollar fine."

Adam was shocked. No prison time? With everything he'd done?

But for the months building up to the final court date, it was almost as if even the prosecution was trying to find a loophole to set Adam free. Virtually everyone involved had a friend or family member who'd been diagnosed with sort form of cancer or HIV. Now, thanks to Adam, that diagnosis meant little more than a trip to the clinic. The world wanted to show its thanks. Even the impassive Judge Eccles seemed pleased. But the judge wasn't finished.

"The only other charge still standing is mutilation of a corpse. Keeping in mind the unusual circumstances of this trial, the court has decided that the decision as to whether or not to press charges should fall to the family of the deceased. In this case, Gene Barfield. If Mr. Barfield does not file the appropriate motions within forty days, the defendant is free and clear."

***

Gene heard the verdict on the news and immediately turned off the television. So it was up to him whether or not Adam was sent to prison?

His first instinct was to let him fry. He had wronged Gene in every way a person could be wronged. He'd lied to him about where he came from, poked and prodded him all his life, even stolen little bits of blood ever since Gene was a baby. He'd turned him into an international case study, completely alone in time and place. His life would never be normal. Never be free.

But…he would still be alive.

He thought back to Nandita in her little village in India. He thought of his dharma. The life debt he owed her. The same life debt he owed Adam. A debt that had to be paid in full before he could move on and be free.

With a strength and wisdom that harkened to another time, Gene took a deep breath and picked up the phone.

***

"Adam? Adam, it's your lawyer. Pick up the phone. Fine—don't pick up the phone. But turn on the TV. You're not going to want to miss this."

Adam cast a weary glare at his answering machine before flipping on the television. There, standing on the steps of the courthouse and looking incredibly grown up in his best suit, was Gene. There were tired circles under his eyes as if he hadn't been sleeping, but other than that, he was steady and calm. He had a page of notes in his hand, but he didn't need them. Instead, he turned to the throng of reporters and said in a loud, clear voice, "I, on behalf of my father…am not pressing charges."

The crowd erupted, but one of the reporters raised his voice loud enough to be heard. "When you say your father, who do you mean?"

There was a brief pause before Gene looked right into the camera.

"Otzi."

If there was one thing Adam learned from his experience, it was that life goes on.

The gossip lessened, the crowds thinned, and slowly, life was able to return to normal.

Well…not quite normal.

Adam looked at the two envelopes on his desk. One was a letter from the Nobel Foundation. It looked thin, too thin to hold good news, but how did one judge these things? The other was a notice of divorce from Maren. She and Sophie were moving to Santa Barbara to be closer to her family, while Gene was renting an apartment of his own in the city.

For the first time in months, all the Barfields were back under the same roof. But it was only for the night.

***

As Maren and Sophie packed up their things into boxes, Gene wandered back down the hall to his old room. His computer was still there, along with his unfinished research paper on Otzi. Given the circumstances, Professor Shields had excused him from completing it. He sat down at his desk with an ironic smile and looked at his latest page of notes.

"Otzi's skin was decorated with fifty-nine separate tattoos."

Gene scoffed. And he wasn't even allowed to get one. His thoughts travelled to Adam, alone in his study just twenty feet away. He supposed he was allowed to get one now.

***

Adam sat down in his chair, relaxed his tired muscles, and took stock.

At that very moment, his wife was packing her things to leave him forever. His children wouldn't speak to him. The scientific community had labeled him a pariah. And he would go down in history not as a savior of the world, but as the man who mutilated a mummy to raise its son.

But despite everything going on around him, Adam almost had to smile.

It was *over*.

The feeling of relief was overpowering, and he realized as he rocked back and forth in his chair that he felt a strange sense of gratitude. He thought of Gene, sitting in his room just a stone's throw away, and felt no sorrow. No despair.

Only pride. A fierce sense of pride.

***

Gene was scrolling down through his lists of information when he suddenly got to a part he hadn't read before. In fact, he didn't remember finding it. He frowned and leaned closer.

Seven men associated with the Iceman or his discoverers have already met their death. There is no explanation for these coincidental fatalities, other than the mysterious way in which they are all connected. Already people are talking about the "Curse of Otzi" in the same breath as the "Curse of King Tut."

***

Adam leaned back in his chair, closing his eyes with a feeling of deep contentment. His hand moved almost of its own accord, and with the same inexplicable impulse that had caused him to touch Otzi to begin with, he reached into the center drawer of his desk. The one he never used.

***

Gene sat back up with a start. A strange chill raised the hairs on the back of his neck, and he found himself calling, "Dad?"

There was a single gunshot.

An explosion of sound shattered the frozen silence of the little house. It echoed off the walls and mirrors before losing itself in the peaceful summer breeze.

Then all was quiet once more.

Before You Go...

Share your voice and help guide other readers to these wonderful books. Even if it's only a line or two your reviews help readers discover the author's books so they can continue creating stories that you'll love. Login to your favorite retailer and leave a review. Thank you.

About the Author

Mary Riesbol June is the mother of five children, including famed cancer researcher Carl June. Born in 1934 during an Oklahoma dust storm, Mary spent the next forty years rearing her family, and medaled in a national poetry contest before finishing Otzi's Curse, her first full length novel.

www.ingramcontent.com/pod-product-compliance
Lightning Source LLC
Chambersburg PA
CBHW022100170626
46808CB00002B/516